# CLASSIC
# HORSE
# & PONY
## STORIES

A DK PUBLISHING BOOK

Produced by Leapfrog Press Ltd.
**Senior Editor** Naia Bray-Moffatt
**Art Editors** Miranda Kennedy
Adrienne Hutchinson
**Picture Research** Liz Moore
**Additional Illustrations** Rob McCaig
John Woodcock

For Dorling Kindersley
**Senior Editor** Alastair Dougall
**Managing Art Editor** Jacquie Gulliver
**Production** Erica Rosen
**US Editor** Gary Werner

First published in Great Britain in 1999 by
Dorling Kindersley Limited, 9 Henrietta Street,
London WC2E 8PS
Visit us on the World Wide Web at
www.dk.com
Copyright © 1999 Dorling Kindersley Limited

First American Edition, 1999
10 9 8 7 6 5 4 3 2 1

Published in the United States by
DK Publishing, Inc.
95 Madison Avenue
New York, New York 10016

DK Publishing books are available at special discounts for bulk
purchases for sales promotions or premiums. Special editions, including
personalized covers, excerpts of existing guides, and corporate imprints
can be created in large quantities for specific needs. For more
information, contact Special Markets Dept./DK Publishing, Inc./95
Madison Ave./New York, NY 10016/Fax:800-600-9098

Library of Congress Cataloging-in-Publication Data
Classic horse & pony stories : the world's best horse and pony stories
  in their real-life settings / chosen by Diana Pullein-Thompson :
  illustrated by Neal Puddephatt
      p.  cm.
   Summary: A collection of classic stories, both realistic and
fanciful, about horses and ponies.
   ISBN 0-7894-4896-3
   1. Horses Juvenile fiction. 2. Ponies Juvenile fiction.
   3. Children's stories. [1. Horses Fiction.  2. Ponies Fiction.
   3. Short stories.] I. Pullein-Thompson, Diana.  II. Puddephatt,
Neal. Ill. III. Title:  Classic horse and pony stories.
PZ5.C562 1999
[Fic] dc21                            99-26011
                                                CIP
Color reproduction by Bright Arts in Hong Kong
Printed by L.E.G.O. in Italy

# CLASSIC
# HORSE
# & PONY
## STORIES

*Selected by*
DIANA PULLEIN-THOMPSON

*Illustrated by*
NEAL PUDDEPHATT

## DK PUBLISHING, INC.

# CONTENTS

# FOREWORD by DIANA PULLEIN-THOMPSON

**W**ild and free, cherished and admired, trained and sick, we meet horses in all kinds of situations in this anthology: Spanish ponies shipwrecked on their way to work in the gold mines of Peru; a wild Australian mare terrified that people will capture her beloved foal. Flicka, a mustang on the point of death, nursed back to life by a boy; Black, a fiery stallion, heavily handicapped but still battling to win a race after a bad start.

*The story of how Black Beauty is broken in is told on pages 42–46*

*Find out about horses in the New World on page 15*

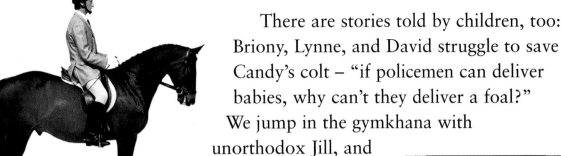

*Fun exercises to improve riding technique are described on page 51*

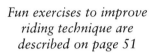

There are stories told by children, too: Briony, Lynne, and David struggle to save Candy's colt – "if policemen can deliver babies, why can't they deliver a foal?" We jump in the gymkhana with unorthodox Jill, and join John and Tess in rescuing noble cart horses from the knacker's yard. Myth and humor have long been part of the horse world. So we read of Pegasus the great winged horse, who carries a hero over dark mountains and deep seas until he finds and kills the deadly Chimera. We laugh with Lewis Carroll's Alice as she watches a ridiculous knight's hopeless attempts to ride a live horse when he really needs a wooden one on wheels.

*Basic health care is discussed on page 81*

*Jill's exciting day at the gymkhana is described on pages 82–90*

I hope you will enjoy these very different and exciting stories. Most of all, I hope that when you put down the book you will have a greater understanding of the true nature of those most lovable of animals, the horse and the pony.

# LIVE CARGO!

from *Misty of Chincoteague* by Marguerite Henry

*The story of how horses arrived in North America – and ran wild.*

A wild, ringing neigh shrilled up from the hold of the Spanish galleon. It was not the cry of an animal in hunger. It was a terrifying bugle, an alarm call.

The captain of the Santo Cristo strode the poop deck. "Cursed be that stallion," he muttered under his breath as he stamped forward and back, forward and back.

Suddenly he stopped short. The wind! It was dying with the sun. It was spilling out of the sails, causing them to quiver and shake. He could feel his flesh creep with the sails. Without wind he could not get to Panama. And if he did not get there, and get there soon, he was headed for trouble. The Moor ponies to be delivered to the Viceroy of Peru could not be kept alive much longer. Their hay had grown musty. The water casks were almost empty. Now came this sudden calm, this heavy warning of a storm.

He plucked nervously at his rusty black beard, as if that would help him think. "We live in the latitude of white squalls," he said, a look of vexation on

*Cupping his hands to his mouth, he bellowed orders.*

his face. "When the wind dies, it will strike with fury." His steps quickened. "We must shorten sail," he said.

Cupping his hands to his mouth, he bellowed orders: "Furl the topgallant sail! Furl the coursers and the main-topsail. Shorten the fore-topsail!"

The ship burst into action. From forward and aft all hands came running. They fell to work furiously, carrying out orders.

Meanwhile, in the dark hold of the ship, a small

*The ship burst into action. From forward and aft all hands came running.*

bay stallion was pawing the floor of his stall. His iron shoes with their sharp rims and turned-down heels threw a shower of sparks, and he felt strong charges of electricity. His nostrils flared at the moisture in the air and the charges of electricity! These were storm warnings – things he knew. An inner urge told him that he must get his mares to high ground before the storm broke. He tried to escape, charging against the chest board of his stall again and again. He threw his head back and bugled.

From stalls beside him and from stalls opposite him, nineteen heads with brown eyes whited. Nineteen young mares caught his anxiety. They, too, tried to escape, rearing and plunging, rearing and plunging.

But soon the animals were no longer hurling themselves. They were being hurled. The ship was pitching and tossing to the rising swell of the sea, flinging the ponies forward against their chest boards, backward against the ship's sides.

A cold wind spiraled down the hatch. It whistled and screamed above the rough voice of the captain. It gave way only to the deep boom of the thunder.

The sea became a wildcat now, and the galleon her prey. She stalked the ship and drove it off course. She slapped at it, rolling her victim from side to side.

Suddenly the galleon shuddered. From bow to stern came an endless rasping sound. The ship had struck a shoal. And with a ripping and crashing of timber the hull cracked open. In that split second the captain, his men, and his live cargo were washed into the boiling foam.

The wildcat sea yawned. She swallowed the men. Only the captain and fifteen ponies managed to come up again. The captain bobbed alongside the stallion and made a wild grasp for his tail, but a giant wave swept him out of reach.

The stallion neighed encouragement to his mares who were struggling to keep afloat, fighting the wreckage and the sea. For long minutes they thrashed about helplessly; and just when their strength was nearly spent, the storm died as suddenly as it had risen.

The sea was no longer a wildcat. She became a kitten, fawning and lapping about the ponies' legs. Now their hooves touched land. They were able to stand! They were scrambling up the beach, up on Assateague Beach, that long, sandy island which shelters the tidewater country of Virginia and Maryland. They were far from the mines of Peru.

The ponies were exhausted, and their coats were heavy with water; but they were free, free, free! They raised their heads and snuffed the wind. The smell was unlike that of the lowland moors of Spain, but it was good! They sucked in the sharp, sweet pungence of pine woods; and somewhere mixed in with the piney smell came the enticing scent of salt grass.

*In that split second the captain, his men, and his live cargo were washed into the boiling foam.*

*They seemed unable to believe that the
island was their own. Not a human
being anywhere. Only grass. And sea.
And sky. And the wind.*

The stallion's hunger stirred him into action. He rounded up his
mares, and with only a watery moon to light the way, he drove them
through the needle-carpeted woods. The mares stopped to eat the leaves
of some myrtle bushes, but the stallion jostled them into line. Then he
took the lead. Through bramble and thicket, through brackish pools of
water, he led the way.

The moon was high overhead when the little band came out on grassy
marshland. They stopped a moment to listen to the wide blades
of grass whisper and squeak in the wind, to sniff the tickling smell of
salt grass.

This was it! This was the exciting smell that had urged them on. With
wild snorts of happiness they buried their noses in the long grass. They
bit and tore great mouthfuls – frantically, as if they were afraid it might
not last. Oh, the salty goodness of it! Not bitter at all, but juicy-sweet
with rain. It was different from any grass they knew. It billowed and
shimmered like the sea. They couldn't get enough of it.

The ponies forgot the forty days and forty nights in the dark hold of the Spanish galleon. They forgot the musty hay. They forgot the smell of bilge water, of oil and fishy odors from the cooking galley.

When they could eat no more, they pawed shallow wells with their hooves for drinking water. Then they rolled in the wiry grass, letting out great whinnies of happiness. They seemed unable to believe that the island was their own. Not a human being anywhere. Only grass. And sea. And sky. And the wind.

At last they slept.

The seasons came and went, and the ponies adopted the new land as their own. They learned how to take care of themselves. When summer came, and with it the greenhead flies by day and the mosquitoes by night, they plunged up to their necks in the cool surf. The sea was their friend. Once it had set them free. Now it protected them from their fiercest enemies.

Winter came, and the grass yellowed and dried; but the ponies discovered that close to the roots it was still green and good to eat.

Even when a solid film of ice sealed the land, they did not go hungry. They broke through the ice with their hooves, or went off to the woods to eat the myrtle leaves that stayed green all winter.

Snow was a new experience, too. They blew at it, making little flurries of their own. They tasted it. It melted on their tongues. Snow was good to drink!

*The stallion's hunger stirred him into action.*

If the Spaniards could have seen their ponies now, they would have been startled at their changed appearance. No longer were their coats sleek. They were as thick and shaggy as the coat of any sheepdog. This was a good thing. On bitter days, when they stood close-huddled for comfort, each pony could enjoy the added warmth of his neighbor's coat as well as his own.

*This was it! This was the exciting smell that had urged them on. With wild snorts of happiness they buried their noses in the long grass.*

# NEW WORLD HORSES

In the early 16th century, Europeans set sail to conquer the newly discovered Americas, bringing horses with them. It is possible that some of these horses were shipwrecked and survived to form herds in the wild. European arrivals were the first horses to live in the Americas since their ancestors died out there 10,000 years earlier. They soon bred, and there are 25 million horses living in the Americas today.

**Cortez in Mexico**
In 1518, Spaniard Hernando Cortez arrived to conquer Mexico with 5 mares, 11 stallions, and 600 soldiers. These tough horses trekked 26 miles (42 km) a day and terrified the natives, who had not seen horses before. Cortez said he conquered Mexico because of them.

**Going native**
By the end of the 18th century, Native North Americans were expert horsemen. They rode escaped Spanish horses, called mustangs, meaning "ownerless" in Spanish.

**Go West**
Horses became true American pioneers. In the mid-19th century, they pulled wagons full of white settlers 2,000 miles (3,300 km) from the east of the United States to the west.

**Island life**
The story describes how wild horses came to live on Chincoteague and Assateague islands, off Virginia. It is historically more likely that they were abandoned rather than shipwrecked. They were discovered in the 1920s, and the publication of Marguerite Henry's book in 1947 made them famous. About 200 live on Assateague today.

# BORN IN THE WILD WIND

from *The Silver Brumby* by Elyne Mitchell

*This extract from the first of a hugely successful series captures Elyne Mitchell's wonderful insights into the behavior of wild horses.*

Once there was a dark, stormy night in spring when, deep down in their holes, the wombats knew not to come out, when the possums stayed quiet in their hollow limbs, when the great flying phallangers that live in the mountain forests never stirred. On this night, Bel Bel, the cream brumby mare, gave birth to a colt foal, pale like herself, or paler, in that wild, black storm.

Bel Bel had chosen the birthplace of the foal wisely. He was on springy snowgrass under a great overhang of granite that sheltered them from the driving rain. There he lay, only a pale bundle in the black dark, while Bel Bel licked him clean and nuzzled him. The wind roared and howled through the granite tors above in the Ramshead range, where the snow still lay; but there was no single sound of animal or bird except the mournful howl of a dingo – once, twice, it rang out and its echo answered, weird and wild.

Bel Bel lifted her head at the sound, and her nostrils dilated. From the shadowy mass between her forefeet came a faint nickering cry and she nuzzled him again. She was very alone with her newborn foal, and far from her own herd; but that was how she had felt it must be. Perhaps because of her color. So much more difficult to hide than bay, brown, black, gray, or chestnut, she had always led a hunted life; and when a foal was going to be born she was very nervous and hid herself far away. Of the three foals she had had, this was the only creamy one, like herself.

*On this night, Bel Bel, the cream brumby mare, gave birth to*
*a colt foal, pale like herself, or paler, in that wild, black storm.*

Bel Bel felt a surge of pride, but the pride was followed by fear. Her son would be hunted as she was and as her own cream mother had been before her – hunted by people, since they were so strange looking in the wild herds. And this colt would have another enemy, too. Every stallion would be doubly against him because of his color.

The wind roared and the rain was cold, so cold, as if it would turn to snow. Even with the shelter of the rock, the storm was beating down on them, and the moving darkness was becoming a thing of terror. The howl of the dingo came again. Bel Bel nosed the tiny colt to get up.

He heaved up his head, stuck his long forelegs out in front of him, and gave a little snort of fear. Bel Bel pushed him up till he stood, his feet far apart, long legs trembling. Then she nosed him, wobbling, bending, step by step to the sandy mouth of the cave; and there, just out of the rain, she let him tumble down again.

Soon it would be time to make him drink; but for the moment, out of the wild storm, he could rest. Dawn must come soon, and in this storm there would be no people around to see a cream brumby mare lead her

*Bel Bel nosed the tiny colt to get up. He heaved up his head, stuck his long forelegs out in front of him, and gave a little snort of fear.*

newborn foal through the snowgums to where there would be grass for her to eat and longed-for water to drink. Bel Bel really knew that there would be very few people in the mountains till all the snow had gone and they were driving their herds of red and white cattle; but the fear of humanity was never far from her thoughts.

Dawn came very slowly, showing first the dark outline of the cave mouth against a faintly lighter sky, then, on the hillside below them, reaching long fingers of forest right up to the rocks, the wind-tormented heads of snowgums, driven and lashing as though they must tear themselves up by the roots. The rain had stopped.

Great massive clouds kept racing up over the mountains; but as the light grew strong, the sky began to look as if it was being torn to shreds by the wind. Flying streamers of rain-washed blue sky appeared, and Bel Bel, feeling very hungry herself, decided it was time the foal should drink. The day would be fair enough for a newborn colt to go with his mother to some better pastures.

"I will call you Thowra," she said, waking him with her nose, "because that means wind. In wind were you born, and fleet as the wind you must be if you will live."

On that first day, while the storm blew itself out, Bel Bel did not take Thowra far, only down through the snowgums to a long glade that led to a heather-banked creek where they could drink. That night they went back to the opening of the cave and the foal slept on the dry sand curled up against his mother's flank.

The next day she decided to take him farther – to a wide, open field in the snowgum forest where the grass grew very sweetly, and where the creek ran shallow over a sand and mica bottom.

The storm had died during the night and there was warm spring sunshine. Bel Bel noticed with pride how the foal trotted more strongly by her side. She did not hurry him, often stopping to graze as they moved under the snowgums or in the long glades. She never left the shelter of the trees without first pausing and looking carefully into the open country ahead. Thus it was through a curtain of the leathery snowgum leaves that she looked out onto the wide sunny field, and saw a bay brumby grazing in the distance by the creek.

Bel Bel became completely still, watching. Then she recognized the bay as a mare of her own herd – Mirri, who had been caught by a stockman as a yearling and managed to get free. Mirri, for this reason, was very cautious around people, and she and Bel Bel had often run together, away from the herd, when they thought the others were getting too close to the stockmen's huts.

Now Bel Bel made out a dark shape near Mirri and knew that the bay mare, too, had had her foal. Unafraid, she led Thowra out to join them.

*She looked out onto the wide sunny field and saw a bay brumby grazing in the distance by the creek.*

When Mirri saw them coming she gave a whinny of greeting. Bel Bel arched her neck a little and stepped proudly beside her creamy son, thinking how his mane and tail were silver and would some day look like spray from a waterfall as he galloped.

Mirri was pleased to see her.

"Well met, Bel Bel," she said, "and what a fine foal you have – creamy, too! I must stir my sleepy-head to show him off!" And she nosed the bright bay at her feet.

The bay raised his head sleepily; but seeing strangers, he became wide awake and struggled to his feet.

"A fine intelligent head," Bel Bel said. "What do you call him?"

"Storm," Mirri answered. "He was born in the worst of the weather, two nights ago. And yours?"

"Thowra, for the wind. He was born then, too. They will be great friends for a year or so." Both mothers nodded wisely, for it was the way of the wild horses that the young colts should run together after they left their dams and until they had reached the age and strength to fight for a mare or two of their own.

Storm and Thowra sniffed at each other curiously, and then both turned back to their mothers for a drink.

Sunny spring days came and the grass grew fresh, green, and sweet. The two mares stayed in Snowgrass Plain, eating, basking in the sun, drinking the cold, clear water, growing strong and sleek after the hard winter, and giving their foals plenty of milk. The foals grew strong, too, and romped and galloped, and rolled in the sun.

Soon they learned to recognize the great wedge-tail eagles floating in the blue arch of sky above them and the call of kurrawongs. They also were unafraid of the friendly gray kangaroos or little brown wallabies.

The two foals were equal in strength and size; and when they were able to follow their mothers for quite a distance, Bel Bel and Mirri, who had become restless to rejoin the herd, started moving off to the south.

For an hour or so they traveled across the ridge-tops in the fringe of the snowgums, and by mid-morning they came out on an immense open

*Sunny spring days came and the grass grew fresh, green, and sweet.*

hillside, which was half of a great basin in the hills. Bel Bel and Mirri checked the foals at the edge of the tree line.

"Never run out into clear country without first taking a very good look," they warned.

The foals could see nothing except steep snowgrass and rocks dropping down beyond their sight and away over a rough, timbered hillside.

"That's where we will spend some of the summer," Bel Bel said. "It is too rough for the men and their cattle, but we get a good picking there."

Neither Thowra nor Storm knew what she meant.

"Down there," said Mirri, "is the Crackenback River. A nice, cool stream to drink at on hot days, and good sandy beaches, in places, for young ones to roll."

They moved out onto the clear hillside, but never went far from the shelter of the trees. Thowra and Storm were too pleasantly tired to want to play and soon dropped to sleep in the sunshine. Bel Bel and Mirri grazed contentedly, a little distance off. All was quiet. There was the far-off sound of the river, running full and strong with water from the melted snows, and the sounds of kurrawongs, but otherwise a profound silence. Even the mares had grown sleepy, when all of a sudden there was a shrill whinny of fear from Thowra.

Bel Bel whipped around in time to see Thowra and Storm leaping up from their sleep. There, grabbing at Thowra as he leapt, was a man. She neighed, calling her foal to come quickly, and started galloping toward them, ready to strike at the man. The foals, with long legs flailing, were racing toward her, wild with fear.

She heard Mirri scream with rage behind her. Then the man turned and ran into the trees.

The mares stopped in their headlong chase to snuff their trembling foals all over and make sure they were unhurt.

Bel Bel was all for chasing the man.

"He was no stockman, he had no whip," she said.

"No," answered Mirri, "but even a man alone, walking through the mountains, sometimes has a gun. No, we will thankfully take our foals and go." She turned to Storm. "See, my son, that was a man. Never go near them, nor their huts, nor their yards where they fence in cattle and their own tame horses. They will hurt you and capture you, put straps of leather rope upon your head, tie you up, fence you in, beat you if you bite or kick…" She was sweating with fear as she spoke, and the two foals' trembling increased.

"And you, Thowra," said Bel Bel. "I told you you would have to be as fleet as the wind. They will hunt you for your creamy coat and your silver mane, so that they may ride astride your back over your own mountains. Beware of Humanity!"

Still sweating with fear, the two mares led their foals away, slipping like wraiths between the trees, trotting steeply down, trotting, trotting.

After quite a long way they were getting near the head of the stream. Here the mares went more slowly, stopping to sniff the air.

"It is from this hut he must have come, but he is not back yet," Bel Bel said.

"There may be others," Mirri's nostrils were quivering.

"I can smell no fresh smoke."

"But, still, let us drop much lower down and cross the stream there, rather than follow the track near the hut."

Bel Bel rubbed one ear on a foreleg.

"The foals are very tired," she said. "We had better spend the night near water. A drink for us will make more milk for them, too."

They slept that evening well below the head of the Crackenback, with the singing stream beside them. But occasionally, when the north wind blew, the two mares would wrinkle their nostrils and mutter between their teeth, "Smoke!" So when the moon rose, they nosed the foals up on their tired legs and started the long climb up Dead Horse Ridge.

*Bel Bel whipped around in time to see Thowra and Storm leaping up from their sleep. There, grabbing at Thowra as he leapt, was a man.*

Once on top they could afford to rest again, but it took the poor foals hours to climb it; and when they found a soak of water to drink, just beyond the top, the mares let the little ones drop down on the soft ground and sleep undisturbed till daybreak.

From there on the traveling was easy, and Bel Bel and Mirri were not so anxious. They were a long way from the hut, and getting very close to the wild horses' winter and spring grazing grounds where, until the snows had all gone, they were never bothered by men.

It was evening when the four of them looked down into a narrow valley off the Cascades and saw their own herd grazing. Just then the great golden chestnut stallion, leader of the herd, raised his head and saw them and let out a shrill trumpeting cry of greeting.

The two mares neighed in reply and started trotting down the long slope, followed by their nervous foals.

*It was evening when the four of them looked down into a narrow valley off the Cascades and saw their own herd grazing.*

# WILD HORSES

Herds of wild horses roam free in many parts of the world – from mustangs on America's vast plains, to Asiatic wild horses on the central Asian steppes, to Brumbies in the Australian outback. Horses were first introduced to Australia in 1788. By 1860, many of these domesticated horses had escaped into the bush and become wild. There are probably as many as 600,000 wild Brumbies in Australia today.

*Brumbies have highly developed survival instincts, including a strong fear of snakes.*

**Going for gold**
After gold was discovered in southeast Australia in 1851, many horse breeders rushed into mining, leaving thousands of abandoned horses to join herds of wild Brumbies.

**On the wild side**
Food was scarce in the bush, and Brumbies became smaller than domestic horses. But they developed a survival instinct that enabled them to withstand their harsh environment.

**Herd instinct**
Like all wild horses, Brumbies live in herds. Each herd is led by a mature stallion, which protects its mares and foals from danger.

**Hunted down**
Stockmen (Australian cowboys) could not tame Brumbies, so tried to hunt them off their lands. By the 1960s the large numbers of Brumbies being killed caused concern worldwide. Today, strict laws limit Brumby hunting.

# PEGASUS

## by Roger Lancelyn Green

*Pegasus was the winged horse of Prince Bellerophon. This is the
story of how Bellerophon captured him in order to kill the Chimera,
a monster with a lion's head, a goat's body, and a dragon's tail.*

After many, many days he [Bellerophon] came to the island where the wise man Polyidus lived, and begged him to reveal how the Chimera might be overcome.

"My son," said Polyidus solemnly, "there is no man walking on the ground who can come near to the Chimera and live, nor is there any four-footed creature on earth."

"Well then," exclaimed Bellerophon in dismay, "only the birds can come near it, and there is no bird strong enough for me to ride on."

"No bird," said Polyidus, "but there is the hippogryph – the flying horse – a great white steed with wings whose home is upon the magic mountain where the nine singing Fairies, called Muses, have their home. Only if you can catch and ride the hippogryph, whose name is Pegasus, can you overcome the Chimera. And even so, you must remember that no weapon can pierce him to the heart."

So Prince Bellerophon set sail for the land of Greece; and in time he came to the magic mountain, and found the singing Fairies seated around the moon-shaped spring of water which Pegasus had made with a stamp of his hoof.

They greeted Bellerophon kindly; but when he told them why he had come, they shook their heads and looked grave.

"Pegasus the flying horse does come to drink at this fountain," they said. "But no mortal can ride him, nor do we know of any magic to catch a hippogryph – the fleetest of creatures that tread the earth, and of any that fly through the air."

Bellerophon was in despair. But, nevertheless, he lay down that night beside the magic fountain, hiding among the grass and flowers as best he could, and determined to keep awake to try to catch Pegasus.

In spite of all his efforts, though, he fell into a deep sleep. And as he slept, a vivid dream came to him. He dreamed that he woke, still lying beside the magic fountain, and saw a shining form standing above him – as of a great Queen who wore a shining shield on her arm and a golden helmet on her head. In her hand she carried a bridle made of gold, and this she held out to him, saying: "Do you sleep, you who may be King of Lycia one day? Rather awake, be ready, and take this which I bring you – the charm to tame your steed, on which no other mortal shall ever ride!"

Then Bellerophon really woke, and as he looked around him he saw something glimmering in the grass beside his hand – the golden bridle which he had seen in his dream.

He had scarcely taken it in his hands when he heard the swish of mighty wings, and the great white hippogryph came gliding down in the moonlight until he stood near him, neighing and arching his neck.

*...a great Queen who wore a shining shield on her arm and a golden helmet on her head.*

Then, folding his wings along his sides, he stepped forward and put down his nose into the silver waters of the fountain to drink.

Very cautiously Bellerophon crept forward on his hands and knees until he was right under the outstretched neck. He then quickly slipped the golden bit into the open mouth and, rising to his feet, slid the bridle straps over the snow-white ears. With a quick movement he passed the golden chain under his neck and clipped it into place. Then, as Pegasus tossed his head in the air with a sudden snort, Bellerophon flung the reins back over his head and sprang onto his back.

In a moment they were off the ground and speeding away through the night, far over the dark mountains and the deep seas.

Prince Bellerophon shouted aloud with joy during that great, crazy flight, and Pegasus his winged horse neighed and tossed his head.

At dawn they landed on another hilltop, above an isthmus between two gulfs of the sea.

Here Pegasus stamped with his hoof again, and another fountain gushed out, at which both he and his rider drank.

Then Bellerophon slipped out the bit so that Pegasus could graze, and the great winged horse neighed in a friendly manner and

*Very cautiously Bellerophon crept forward on his hands and knees...*

rubbed his nose against his rider's shoulder.

Now that he had his steed, Prince Bellerophon set out in search of the fierce Chimera. At last he came upon her ravaging through the fruitful valleys, devouring the sheep and cattle, and destroying all that stood in her way with her fiery breath.

Flying high over it in the air, Bellerophon began shooting at the creature with sharp arrows. But although these wounded her, they did not seem able to do her any real harm. They merely made her far more furious and destructive. Roaring loudly, the Chimera bounded around, breathing great tongues of flame through her goat's mouth, which stuck out from a

*Now that he had his steed, Prince Bellerophon set out in search of the fierce Chimera. At last he came upon her.*

long neck from the middle of her back. As he swooped down on Pegasus, Bellerophon felt the heat of that deadly breath, and an idea came to him.

He soared away on Pegasus, and soon came flying back again with a long spear held firmly in both hands, and on the point of it a great lump of lead. Down over the Chimera he swooped on Pegasus, and as the terrible creature opened her goat-mouth to breathe out a great tongue of fire, Bellerophon dropped the lump of lead down her throat.

The Chimera then roared and rolled and writhed on the ground, clawing at herself with her lion's talons and her dragon's claws. The lump of lead melted in her burning throat, and the molten metal went trickling down into her entrails and her stomach, and searing its way through her until it reached her heart.

And then the Chimera rolled over for the last time, and lay still and dead.

*And then the Chimera rolled over for the last time,*
*and lay still and dead.*

# HORSES IN ANCIENT GREEK

Horses not only played an important part in Greek mythology, but they were also central to life in ancient Greece. Pictures of horses and chariots on vases from 1550-1500 BC suggest a society in which the horse was crucial to battle, worship, and sport. However, because of the unsuitable natural environment, the Greeks had to rely on horses from neighboring areas to improve their native breeds.

**Warfare**
In early Greek warfare, horses were used to pull chariots to battle. Later, mounted troops crossed Greece's mountainous terrain.

*The myth of Pegasus emphasises the close relationship between man and horse. Prince Bellerophon can only defeat the Chimera with the help of Pegasus.*

**Sports**
Chariot racing was a national sport in ancient Greece. The first chariot races were for four-horse chariots, and were held at the Olympic Games in 680 BC.

**Worship**
Although the horse itself was not worshiped, its image was used to represent gods and goddesses who were worshiped. This statue of a horse head comes from a temple dedicated to the goddess Demeter, the goddess of women, marriage, and agriculture. She was often represented by a black mare's head.

**Breeding**
The Pindos is directly descended from the old Thessalonian horse bred in ancient Greece. Noted by the Greek poet Oppian (c.AD211), for its "beauty, courage, and endurance," today the pony is used as a pack animal in the mountains, for light farm work, and forestry.

# A FOAL FOR CANDY

from the novel by Diana Pullein-Thompson

*Based on Diana Pullein-Thompson's real experience*
*of witnessing the birth of a horse, this is a moving*
*account of a foal's unexpected arrival into the world.*

I woke up. It was dark. A little rain spattered the window pane. My first thought was for Candy. I turned over and tried to be calm. "Briony checked her at midnight," I told myself. "But we should have brought her to the home field. The vet said…" The house was very quiet. The silence was beautiful in the soft summer night. The rain had stopped now and I could smell the lavender bush which grew at the bottom of my window. For the hundredth time I wished I had a dog lying at the end of my bed or in a basket nearby. I needed a being with whom I could discuss my fears. In this way I might have cleared my mind.

"Half an hour's delay can be as dangerous for a foaling mare as two hours for a cow."

Where had I read that? I turned over again and switched on the light, which immediately attracted a sand-colored moth. I dragged my watch from under my pillow – ten past one. If she foaled disastrously tonight and died I would never forgive myself. It could be that some strange telepathy between Candy and myself had wakened me, a message moving like a spirit across the great darkness of the night. My imagination soared; fearful pictures ran before my mind like a horror film.

My mother once told me that it was the things you hadn't done which you regretted in later life. "Too late," she declared, were the saddest words in the English language. I got up, pulled jeans over my pyjamas, put on a sweater, and crept downstairs. I picked up a heavy

*My mother once told me that it was the things you hadn't done which you regretted in later life.*

rubber-clad flashlight, pushed my bare feet into boots, and slipped out into the cool darkness.

Walking down the lane, I was conscious of charcoal clouds moving across an immeasurable sky, and trees standing still like stones. The world was suddenly a stage waiting for lights, actors, and audience to bring it to life.

"Candy?"

"Are you all right?" I was astonished at my matter-of-fact tone of voice as I trapped Candy in my flashlight's beam and saw her flared nostrils, her wild eyes, and sweat-soaked neck. I held out my arms as though I could catch her in them like a frightened child, but she flung herself at my feet with a groan, her sides heaving, her stomach enormous, her hoofs churning the grass into mud as her panting turned into squeaks which seemed extraordinary coming from so large an animal. I had a picture in my mind from a veterinary book of how a foal should arrive; forelegs first with the head resting on them. Now, looking at Candy, I knew something was wrong. For under the flashlight beam I saw that one hoof was pushing in the wrong place, causing a red, ball-like bulge under her tail. My instinct was to stay and comfort and help her, but common sense made me run. I vaulted the gate, tore down the road, my heart thudding, and reached the house.

"Wake up everyone! Candy is foaling and everything's going wrong – everything." There was a trace of panic in my voice, because as usual I feared the worst. Briony keeps the vet's number on a card for emergencies, so I soon got through to the office, where a recording instructed me where to phone to reach the vet on duty. Next I had to look up a code, and by the time I had done that, David, my brother, and Briony were downstairs putting on shoes.

Sleepily, Thelma Wright, our nicest vet, said she would come at once. I grabbed a headcollar and tore back to the field with Briony following with sterilized string and scissors, in case the umbilical cord needed tying and cutting.

Candy was lying on the ground with her teeth bared.

"She could die," I said dramatically.

"Calm down!" cried my sister. "You won't make a vet if you overreact. David, will you please run back and bring a bucket of warm water with antiseptic and the Vaseline if you can find it?

Then our parents arrived.

"She looks in a bad way," Mother said.

"She could die," I repeated. "Foaling mares die more easily than calving cows. I've read it."

"We're more likely to lose the foal than the mare," my sister told me. "I wish David would hurry."

"And Thelma Wright. What on earth is Thelma Wright doing?" I asked, kneeling down by Candy's head.

"Better fetch Fred," Dad suggested, as those terrible squeaks of pain started again. "He said he worked on a Canadian stud farm."

"She's pushing for all she's worth, but the foal's stuck. There's no time to waste, and he's the only person nearby who might know what to do," Mother agreed.

"But he hates us," I cried seeing again those angry, glittering eyes at the door of the tack room, the gun glinting under his arm. "He thinks I'm a nosy."

"Oh, forget that! Don't hang around or you'll have a dead foal on your hands," Dad said. "Even I can see that, and the mare's in pain."

"Fred may hate you, but he loves animals; there's no doubt about that," Mother added.

"Go on, Lynne," urged Briony.

"No, I'm staying with Candy. I'm scared of Fred. Please go, Briony. Please be quick. I'm sure the foal needs turning around or something."

Briony ran. Candy scrambled to her feet, circled twice, and collapsed on the ground again.

"Labor pains. You've got to expect labor pains," Mother said.

*David came back across the field with a bucket and a hurricane lamp.*

"One hoof must be in the wrong place. They should come out side by side," I explained. "Whoa, Candy! Gently, Candy! Help is coming."

Then David came back across the field with a bucket and a hurricane lamp. "We need more light on the scene. How is she?"

"Terrible. Do you think I could turn the hoof around?"

"No, you could do more damage. Better wait for Briony," Dad said.

"But Briony doesn't know everything," I insisted. "It's all happening too high up."

"She knows more than you," Mother said. "She's older."

"Lynne, you're overdramatizing again," David muttered gently.

"I don't know," Mother said. "She does look rather miserable, and we're standing round like a load of half-wits. If policemen can deliver babies, why can't we deliver the foal?"

"Give me the bucket, please," I cried.

I plunged my hands into the water, put Vaseline on my arms, and did what I had seen a vet do on television, but I couldn't get a hand inside.

*"She does look rather miserable, and we're standing round like a load of half-wits".*

Then Briony came back. "Fred's getting dressed. What are you doing, Lynne? Move over, let me have a go."

She took off her coat, rolled up her sleeves, disinfected her hands, and applied Vaseline but she was no more successful than I had been. "I can't. There seems no room. She closes up on me," she complained.

"Come on now, make way. Where's the soap? We'll soon put things right." Fred had arrived. He flung his coat down. "Hoof pushing against the rectum. Could be serious. Must hurry," he added. "I've turned plenty of foals around in my time. You don't need no vet. Whoa, little lady! Steady there!"

He brought out his hands and washed them in the water. "She'll be all right now. I've straightened the hoof. It's beside its mate now. The birth will be normal."

"Why couldn't I do it?" Briony asked.

"You have to time it right, push in a hand between the heaves. I've turned sheep and cattle, too. It's easy once you know," Fred beamed.

"Here comes the vet," shouted David. "I'll open the gate."

"Late as usual," growled Fred.

"That's not fair," Mother said.

"I went to your house. You should have told me where the mare was," Thelma Wright complained.

"My fault. I'm terribly sorry," I said, chastened.

"Then I saw the lights. I really only lost five minutes."

Now the vet's car lights lit up the whole scene. Candy looked around, her cheeks pinched with pain, her nostrils still flared, milk running from her teats.

"Hoof pushing against rectum. I brought it down. Look, foal's coming now," Fred said, as Thelma Wright sprang from her car.

She took one hoof and Fred the other and, pulling gently, they brought out the foal, long, wet, and dark as the night.

"It's a fine one," Fred said.

After Thelma Wright had injected mare and foal with an antibiotic and anti-tetanus serum, she left to see a sick cow, and we stood in an admiring circle to watch Candy, who prodded her foal with a hoof.

"Don't, you'll hurt him," I objected.

"That's normal, that is. Wants to see what he's made of," Fred told us. "Go on, old lady, get the little devil moving." The next moment Candy was guiding the foal in a circle with her knees.

"He's got to stand before he can suck. Well, I'm going back to my warm bed." Fred turned away.

We looked at each other, searching for words. It's hard to express gratitude to someone for whom you feel no affection.

"We're enormously grateful. You saved the foal," Briony began rather formally. "The vet might have been too late. We can't thank you enough."

"It's not the first and I dare say it won't be the last. You've got a nice colt there, well bred I would say."

"Well, good night," said Mother. "We're all grateful to you. I'm off to bed as well."

"Me too," Dad said. "What a night!"

The adults walked away, apart from Briony, whom we never think of as grown up, but merely as one of us with just a bit more authority.

But our troubles weren't over.

"We've got to get him sucking. The first milk's very important," Briony said. "See if you can guide his mouth to the udder, Lynne."

David held the hurricane lamp so that a shaft of light fell between Candy's hind legs. But when I got the foal's mouth in the right place, he only fumbled clumsily, too weak to draw the milk and too stupid to bend his head in the right direction.

"It's because he's had a difficult birth," my sister announced. "Who in this village has a baby's bottle?"

"Mirabelle's parents' housekeeper has a baby boy," David replied promptly. "I've seen the girl stuff a bottle in the child's mouth when he keeps crying. I'll go and wake Mirabelle if you like."

"It's half past two – an awful time to drag someone out of bed. But we can't leave this little guy without milk," Briony said. "He'll get weaker and weaker if he doesn't take the milk soon. There's not a lot of time. David, do you think…"

"Yes, all right. I'll go, but I just hope I don't wake up Mirabelle's parents."

"We'll leave you in charge, Lynne. Here's the flashlight. We'll take the lamp."

The faint squelch of their feet on the grass died away. The charcoal clouds moved silently across the ink-black sky. Candy lay there, looking like a pale Chinese porcelain horse, with her foal folded up at her side. I wanted to sit down then to share their peacefulness.

Soon David, Mirabelle, and Briony came striding back across the field.

"All sterilized and clean!" Briony waved a baby's plastic bottle. "Up you get, Candy! Come on!" She pushed the cream body with her foot.

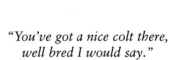

"Oh, what a pity to move them when they look so comfortable," cried Mirabelle. "Why don't you leave them? What a dear little foal! I'm so glad you woke me."

*"You've got a nice colt there, well bred I would say."*

"He must suck or his insides won't function properly," Briony said sternly. Then she started to milk the mare.

After much persuasion, the foal took two pulls from the bottle and then gave up. "Not enough," my sister said. "We must persevere."

So we went on trying until a skein of pale gray unwove its thin strands across the sky, spreading soft light across the darkness.

"He's not going to suck – any fool can see that," David said flatly.

"Well, now it's light I'll call the vet again. There's no other way,"

Briony said.

Half an hour later, Thelma Wright fed the foal by tube. I poured Candy's milk from a plastic jug down a funnel attached to the tube, which had been inserted though the foal's left nostril and ran right down into his stomach.

"There, now. He'll be all right," Thelma Wright said when the jug was empty.

And within minutes, the foal was up and walking on his long, wobbly legs. Soon afterward, the vet removed the tube and the long night was over.

*…Thelma Wright fed the foal by tube. I poured Candy's milk from a plastic jug down a funnel attached to the tube, which had been inserted though the foal's left nostril…*

# A FOAL IS BORN

A mare gives birth to a foal after a pregnancy of about 11 months. She sometimes foals lying down and often at night, like Candy. In a normal birth, the foal's front feet will come out first, then its nose, its head, and shoulders, then the rest follows. Within an hour, the foal will stand and suckle from its mother. The mare will continue to feed her foal for up to a year.

**Foaling box**
Ideally, highly-bred mares, like Candy, should be watched carefully when foaling in case something goes wrong. A foaling box, like this one, can be useful as it provides warmth and light.

*From the sixth month of a mare's pregnancy, it is possible to see the foal's movements inside the mare's swollen belly.*

**First steps**
After the birth, the mother licks her foal clean. Then she encourages the foal to stand. His long legs make it easier for him to reach his mother's milk, but mean that his first steps are a bit wobbly.

*The foal's soft woolly coat, known as milk hair, has now been replaced by an adult coat.*

**Mother's milk**
The first milk is called colostrum and provides important nutrients for the newborn foal. The foal should drink from his mother within the first hour to give him vital strength.

**Five-month-old foal**
By five months, a foal's body will have reached adult proportions. It will not be fully grown until it is five or six years old.

# MY BREAKING IN

from *Black Beauty* by Anna Sewell

*Published in 1877,* Black Beauty *was the first story to be written from a horse's point of view. Never before had readers been given a sense of what it must be like for an animal so dependent on human beings, whether cruel or kind. In this extract, Black Beauty's owner decides it's time his four-year-old started to learn about the realities of life...*

I was now beginning to grow handsome; my coat had grown fine and soft, and was bright black. I had one white foot, and a pretty white star on my forehead. I was thought very handsome; my master would not sell me till I was four years old. He said lads ought not to work like men, and colts ought not to work like horses till they were grown up.

When I was four years old, Squire Gordon came to look at me. He examined my eyes, my mouth, and my legs; and then I had to walk and trot and gallop before him. He seemed to like me, and said, "When he has been well broken in, he will do very well." My master said he would break me in himself, as he should not like me to be frightened or hurt; and he lost no time about it, he began the next day.

*My master said he would break me in himself... and he lost no time about it, he began the next day.*

Every one may not know what breaking in is, so I will describe it. It means to teach a horse to wear a saddle and bridle and carry on his back a man, woman, or child; to go just the way they wish, and to go quietly. Besides this, he has to learn to wear a collar, a crupper, and a breeching, and to stand still while they are put on; then to have a cart or a chaise fixed behind him, so that he cannot walk or trot without dragging it after him. And he must go fast or slow, just as his driver wishes. He must never start at what he sees, nor speak to other horses, nor bite, nor kick, nor have any will of his own; but always do his master's will, even though he may be very tired or hungry. But the worst of all is, when his harness is once on, he may neither jump for joy nor lie down for weariness. So you see this breaking in is a great thing.

I had of course long been used to a halter and a headstall, and to be led around in the field and lanes quietly; but now I was to have a bit and a bridle. My master gave me some oats as usual, and after a good deal of coaxing, he got the bit into my mouth and the bridle fixed. It was a nasty thing! Those who have never had a bit in their mouths cannot think how bad it feels; a great piece of cold, hard steel as thick as a man's finger to be pushed into one's mouth, between one's teeth and over one's tongue, with the ends coming out at the corners of your mouth and held fast there by straps over your head, under your throat, around your nose, and under your chin. And there is no way in the world can you get rid of the nasty hard thing; it is very bad! Yes, very bad! At least I thought so; but I knew my mother always wore one when she went out, and all horses did when they were grown up. So, with the nice oats and my master's pats, kind words, and gentle ways, I got used to wearing my bit and bridle.

Next came the saddle; but that was not half so bad. My master put it on my back very gently, while old Daniel held my head. He then tightened the girths fast under my body, patting and talking to me all the time. Then I had a few oats, then a little leading around, and this he did every day till I began to look for the oats and saddle. At length, one morning my master got on my back and rode me around the meadow on the soft grass. It certainly did feel strange; but I must say I felt rather proud to carry my master. And as he continued to ride me a little every day, I soon became accustomed to it.

The next unpleasant business was putting on the iron shoes; that too was very hard at first. My master went with me to the smith's forge, to see that I was not hurt or got any fright. The blacksmith took my feet in his hand one after the other, and cut away some of the hoof. It did not pain me, so I stood still on three legs till he had done them all. Then he took a piece of iron the shape of my foot and clapped it on. He drove some nails through the shoe and into my hoof, so that the shoe was firmly on. My feet felt very stiff and heavy, but in time I got used to it.

And now having gone so far, my master went on to break me to harness; there were more new things to wear. First, a stiff heavy collar on my neck, and a bridle with great side-pieces against my eyes called blinders. And blinders they were indeed, for I could not see on either side, but only straight in front of me. Next there was a small saddle with a nasty stiff strap that went right under my tail; that was the crupper. I hated the crupper – to have my long tail doubled up and poked through that strap was almost as bad as the bit. I never felt more like kicking, but of course I could not kick such a good master. So, in time, I got used to everything, and could do my work as well as my mother.

*The next unpleasant business was putting on the iron shoes.*

I must not forget to mention one part of my training, which I have always considered a very great advantage. My master sent me for two weeks to a neighboring farm, one with a meadow which was bordered on one side by a railroad. There were some sheep and cows, and I was turned in among them.

I shall never forget the first train that ran by. I was feeding quietly

near the pickets which separated the meadow from the railroad, when
I heard a strange sound at a distance. Before I knew where it came from –
with a rush and a clatter, and a puffing out of smoke – a long black train
of something flew by, and was gone almost before I could draw my
breath. I turned and galloped to the far side of the meadow

*...a long black train of
something flew by, and was
gone almost before I could
draw my breath. I turned
and galloped...*

as fast as I could go; and there I stood snorting with astonishment and fear. In the course of the day many other trains went by, some more slowly. These drew up at the station close by, and sometimes made an awful shriek and groan before they stopped. I thought it very dreadful, but the cows went on eating very quietly, and hardly raised their heads as the frightful black thing came puffing and grinding past.

For the first few days I could not feed in peace; but as I found that this terrible creature never came into the field, or did me any harm, I began to disregard it. Very soon I cared as little about the passing of a train as the cows and sheep did.

Since then I have seen many horses much alarmed and restive at the sight or sound of a steam engine. But thanks to my good master's care, I am as fearless at railroad stations as in my own stable.

Now if anyone wants to break in a young horse well, that's the way.

*Besides this, he has to have a cart or a chaise fixed behind him,
so that he cannot walk or trot without dragging it after him.*

# BREAKING IN

The term "breaking in" a horse is a negative way of describing the taming of the animal as it suggests the spirit of the horse must be broken. When Anna Sewell wrote *Black Beauty*, many cruel methods were used to break a horse's wild spirit. Today, people believe that the most effective way to tame a horse is with patience and understanding. The process is now called "making" a horse.

**Saddle**
The kindest way to get a horse used to the feel of a saddle is to place it on his back without a rider at first.

**Harness**
In Victorian times, working horses like Black Beauty had to learn to wear a harness instead of a saddle, to pull carts or carriages.

**Bridle**
A steel bit and bridle are used to give the rider more control of the horse. Black Beauty finds the bit uncomfortable at first.

**Wearing shoes**
Equipping a horse with metal shoes is done by a blacksmith. The shoes prevent a horse's hooves from being damaged on hard roads.

*Horse shoe and nails*

*A headcollar is used to make handling a horse easier.*

**The gentle touch**
A horse that is treated with gentleness and kindness will always respond better to its rider.

# ALICE AND THE WHITE KNIGHT

From *Alice Through the Looking Glass* by Lewis Carroll

*During her adventures beyond the large mirror in her drawing room, Alice encounters the bumbling White Knight; who promises to escort her through a wood. Alice soon notices that there is something rather odd about him – he seems quite unable to stay on his horse!*

Alice walked on in silence, every now and then stopping to help the poor Knight, who certainly was not a good rider. Whenever the horse stopped (which it did very often), he fell off in front; and whenever it went on again (which it generally did rather suddenly), he fell off behind. Otherwise he kept on pretty well, except that he had a habit of now and then falling off sideways. And, as he generally did this on the side on which Alice was walking, she soon found that it was the best plan not to walk quite so close to the horse.

"I'm afraid you've not had much practice in riding," she ventured to say, as she was helping him up from his fifth tumble.

The Knight looked very much surprised, and a little offended, at the remark. "What makes you say that?" he asked, as he scrambled back into the saddle, keeping hold of Alice's hair with one hand, to save himself from falling over on the other side.

"Because people don't fall off so often, when they've had practice."

"I've had plenty of practice," the Knight said very gravely, "plenty of practice!"

Alice could think of nothing better to say than "Indeed?" but she said it as heartily as she could. They went on a little way in silence after this, the Knight with his eyes shut, muttering to himself, and Alice watching anxiously for the next tumble.

"The great art of riding," the Knight suddenly began in a loud voice, waving his right arm as he spoke, "is to keep . . ." Here the sentence ended as suddenly as it had begun, as the Knight fell heavily on the top of his head exactly in the path where Alice was walking. She was quite frightened this time, and said in an anxious tone as she picked him up, "I hope no bones are broken?"

"None to speak of," the Knight said, as if he didn't mind breaking two or three of them. "The great art of riding, as I was saying, is to keep your balance properly. Like this, you know . . ."

He let go the bridle and stretched out both his arms to show Alice what he meant. This time he fell flat on his back, right under the horse's feet.

*"The great art of riding, as I was saying,*
*is to keep your balance properly."*

*"Plenty of practice!" he went on repeating.*

"Plenty of practice!" he went on repeating, all the time that Alice was getting him on his feet again. "Plenty of practice!"

"It's too ridiculous!" cried Alice, losing all her patience this time. "You ought to have a wooden horse on wheels, that you ought!"

"Does that kind go smoothly?" the Knight asked in a tone of great interest, clasping his arms around the horse's neck as he spoke, just in time to save himself from tumbling off again.

"Much more smoothly than a live horse," Alice said, with a little scream of laughter, and in spite of all she could do to prevent it.

"I'll get one," the Knight said thoughtfully to himself. "One or two – several."

*"You ought to have a wooden horse on wheels, that you ought!"*

# BASIC RIDING TECHNIQUE

Despite his inability to stay "on board," the White Knight is right about the essential art of riding: keeping your balance. When you learn to ride, your first lesson will probably concentrate purely on your "seat" – the way you sit in your saddle. It's not as easy as it looks, but there are many exercises that you can do to give you confidence in the saddle, and help you keep your balance.

**Sitting in the saddle**
The correct position for a well-balanced seat is to sit deep in the saddle, back straight, head up, thighs and knees pressed down.

**Around the world**
This is a very good exercise for learning how to keep your balance in the saddle. First, holding on to the saddle, swing your right leg over the front of the saddle, so you face sideways. Next, move your left leg over the back of the saddle so you face the pony's tail. Continue until you face forwards again.

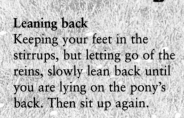

**Leaning back**
Keeping your feet in the stirrups, but letting go of the reins, slowly lean back until you are lying on the pony's back. Then sit up again.

**Swinging arms**
With your feet in the stirrups, lift up your arms to shoulder level. Then turn your body from the waist to one side, then the other.

**Toe touching**
In this exercise you lean down to touch your left foot with your right hand and then your right foot with your left hand.

# THE CHAMPIONS

## by Monica Edwards

*Nowadays draft horses are sadly becoming a rarer and
rarer sight. In this story, Tess and John try to raise
enough money to save two prize-winning Shire horses,
Flower and Captain, from the slaughterhouse.*

John Thatcher and his sister Tess were running down the track to
Manor Farm. It was not to see the farmer, who wasn't the sort of
man anybody would see on purpose, or to see his wife, who was
chronically sad. They were looking for Walter Pooley, the horseman.

"If only it hadn't been for school," John was saying as they ran,
"we could have watched the plowing match ourselves. I wonder why
they always hold it during the school term?"

"I'll bet Walter won his class, anyway," Tess said, "and the
championship, too. He nearly always has, as well as dozens in other
places."

"But it gets more difficult every year, with all the modern hydraulic-
lift tractors. Walter's almost the only horse team left," John said.

They climbed the gate into the farmyard and crossed a stretch of
concrete to the stable. It was quite clearly a stable, because of the halter
thrown over the open half-door, and the sounds and smells of horses
coming out of it. The powerful, brown hind view of one of its inhabitants
filled the doorway like a picture in a frame.

"Hey there, young uns," said Walter Pooley. He had one hand, with a
curry comb in it, resting on a gray horse's rump. The other was grooming
its flank in long, strong strokes that sent fine dust floating in a shaft of
low sunlight.

*The powerful, black hind view of one of its inhabitants
filled the doorway like a picture in a frame.*

"Hello Walter!" said Tess and John, looking around at the shining bridles where they hung on pegs along the wall. On one of them a crisp, red rosette was tied. But far more important than this, there was a new card at the end of the row of prize cards that were tacked underneath the bridles; it said, "Champion; Finkley and District Plowing Match."

"Walter! You've won it again!"

"That's right, Flower and Captain's won it again. Dah! Those stinking tractors haven't got nothing on a real pair of horses,"

*"Those stinking tractors haven't got nothing
on a real pair of horses," said Walter proudly.*

said Walter proudly. But there was a kind of sadness in the pride in his voice. John thought it was sadness for the passing of the heyday of great horses. He said, "Well anyway, there'll always be a rear horse team while you and Flower and Captain are around," to cheer Walter up.

"Ah," said Walter non-committally. "This one made the 99th prize and the eleventh championship, all with Flower and Captain. Pity it's the last match this year, ain't it, Flower, old girl? I'd like to've made the century; and even better, the dozen."

"You'll easily do it next year," Tess said. "May I give them a sugar lump each for winning? And one for Prince, to make it fair."

"Carry on," said Walter, moving over with his brushes and curry comb to Captain, who was a perfect match for Flower except that his dappling was a little darker, and his build a little heavier. "But as to next year, who's to know where me and the horses'll be? Manor Farm's been sold, just like that, over all our heads and no warning."

"Walter – no!" Tess and John stared at him.

"I seen the new man down here two or three times, never dreaming what he were here for. But the boss, he tells me they clinched the deal this morning, while I were plowing."

"But can't you stay on with the new man – you and the horses?" John asked. "I should think he'd be glad to have a champion plowman and a team like this."

"That's just where you're mistaken, son." Walter was brushing out Captain's silver main, still crinkly from the morning's festive plaits. "The new gent's mechanical. He don't hold with horses and that – like most of 'em today."

"Perhaps whoever buys the horses will take you on with them," John suggested. "They aren't likely to have a better plowman."

Walter looked up at them starkly, over Captain's broad back. "No one buys horses much these days, least of all old horses. Prince, there, he'll likely go to some smallholder chap – he's young and useful. But Flower and Captain, they're rising 15 now; and they never worked for nobody but me. They wouldn't go kindly for a new horseman now, at their time of life."

Tess wiped her sugar-slobbery palm on a handful of straw. "But surely someone will pay something for Flower and Captain? Someone who sees what fine, beautiful horses they are, and who would be proud to have champions like them."

"Ah. Someone'll pay, you bet. And that'll be the slaughter merchants. Fine, big horses is what they like above anything."

John and Tess simply didn't believe what Walter said. They thought he was exaggerating out of bitterness for what was going to happen. But Walter shook his head sadly. He brought his large hand down with a tender slap on Captain's rump and said: "We got about one month, me and the horses. Me to find another job – who wants a horseman, nowadays? – and the horses… well… Anyway," he added firmly, "they've had a good life. A good, long, useful life, and all the while they carried flying colors."

"But it mustn't happen!" Tess said. "We'll have to do something – I don't

*"Couldn't Flower and Captain retire? They surely deserve it, if any horses ever did."*

know what, but there must be something. If they're too old and weak for anybody but you, Walter, what about a retirement home for horses? Couldn't Flower and Captain retire? They surely deserve it, if any horses ever did."

Walter nodded solemnly. "I daresay. I thought about that myself, but I reckon you got to pay to put horses in retirement. And another thing, even supposing some home did offer to take 'em, can you see the boss letting 'em go, and not getting a penny back when those slaughterhouses will put up around 40 or 50 quid apiece?"

*"We got about one month, me and the horses. Me to find another job – who wants a horseman, nowadays?"*

The beam of sunlight had gone from the stable window and soon it would be dusk. John and Tess patted the horses and picked up their satchels. "Cheer up Walter! Something will happen, I'm sure it will. We'll let you know the moment we've thought of anything."

But they couldn't do that, because when they thought of it they were on the bus on the way to school the next morning. "What we've got to do," John said, "is collect money for buying the horses and paying for their retirement."

"But how much? And who from?" Tess replied.

"We'll find out how much. I'll write to one of the homes. Then we'll have to try everyone we know, and start a Save the Horses Fund."

For the next few days they had no time at all for visiting the farm, except for one brief dash in and out to tell Walter the wonderful news that the Horses' Home had written to say that they would accept Flower and Captain for nothing at all, if necessary.

"Oh dear, it simply must be, now we've said so," Tess said anxiously.

But by the end of the first week the fund stood at only £15 2s. John and Tess went up to the farm on the Saturday morning to tell Walter that they were still pushing on.

"We must reach £80 somehow; and we're going to, no matter how unlikely it looks now." Walter looked at them gravely over Captain's steaming back. The horses had just come in from the fields and were being unharnessed for the dinner hour.

"Look, young uns," he said gently, "you better forget that fund, see. You can't make it now. The boss, he fixed up with the slaughter men. £45 for Captain here and £40 for Flower. Saturday noon."

"Oh Walter! But that's only a week away." Walter nodded, saying nothing. But after a minute he said suddenly and fiercely, "I won't let 'em have my horses, though. My horses won't go through their murder sheds." He looked at the three of them, the brown and the grays, lovingly. "That Prince, he's all right! Going to the brewery. But my grays…"

"What are you going to do, Walter?" Tess looked at him half hopefully, half apprehensively.

"I got me own gun," said Walter, with a strange kind of dignity. "I won't let 'em suffer. Sooner put 'em down myself merciful, I would, than let those pirates get a hand on them. And they can do what they like to me, afterward. My horses've served me all their lives, and now I stand to serve them."

John and Tess were very shaken. Their chances of raising enough money to outbid the slaughtererhouse before the following Saturday were almost hopeless.

*Then suddenly, during breakfast on Tuesday morning, the children's mother said, "You could try writing to the paper perhaps."*

"There must be a way," said John, "if only we can think of it."

But no one they knew seemed to be any better than they were at thinking of it. And the next two days at fund-raising work only added a further £3 10s to the fund, though everyone at both John's and Tess's schools had done their best.

Then suddenly, during breakfast on Tuesday morning, the children's mother said, "You could try writing to the paper perhaps."

"The paper? Gosh, yes, I guess we could!" John said. "But do you think they'd put it in? Would many people help us if they did? I mean, Walter and the horses would be strangers to them."

But when they met in the bus coming home that evening, John said to Tess: "I wrote that letter to the paper. If they put it in and anyone answers, we'll get the letters on Saturday morning."

"But Saturday morning is..." Tess began uncertainly. Then, "John! Listen! We must go to the  farm at once and tell Walter to wait until after the post before, before..." her voice failed.

"At least an hour after the post, to give us time to get to the farm," John said. "But of course, the paper might not print my letter."

The paper did print it. John and Tess could hardly concentrate at all on Friday's lessons, wondering whether enough people could possibly, at that moment, be writing out enough checks and postal orders to save the horses.

On Saturday morning the postman came up the path as usual and put two letters through the mailbox. They were both ordinary business circulars. John and Tess simply couldn't look at each other. Finishing breakfast was quite out of the question. Neither of them had felt so awful in all their lives. The morning began its heavy-footed, slow progress, until it was nearly three-quarters of an hour after the postman's visit. Tess wouldn't look at the clock, but John was looking at it all the time. Tess just stared hopelessly out of the window. And that was why she saw the red van first. It pulled up outside their gate, behind the hedge, and she could see a postman's cap bobbing along toward the doors at the back of the van.

*"A whole sack! Look, Tess. A sackful of letters, just for us!"*

"John – it's a post office van!" she hardly dared hope. But John, dashing across to the window, felt that he had known all along that help must be coming – if only it came in time.

"A whole sack! Look, Tess. A sackful of letters, just for us!" They tore through the room and down the hall and opened the door.

"Too many for the postman's bicycle," grinned the man with the sack. "What've you started, then? A mail order business."

It was fifty minutes from the time of the first postman's visit. John's usually slow brain jumped to the only answer. "I say, sir! Could you possibly take the sack, and us with it, to Manor Farm? Now, sir? You see, it's a matter of life and death."

"We can explain everything on the way," pleaded Tess.

The driver looked at them. "Right. Hop in," he said. "It's against regulations, but with life and death you've got to make allowances."

In less than two minutes John had him breaking further regulations, because he had never driven that van so fast before, in all his 12 years at the post office. Even up the bumpy road to Manor Farm they hardly slowed down. In the farmyard they threw themselves out as the van came to a stop and raced across the concrete to the stable.

"Walter!"

He was tying a white cloth around Flower's eyes.

"Walter! We've got a whole sackful of letters here, and probably every one with money in it. They came late, because there were so many. We brought them as quickly as we could."

Walter turned toward them with a slow, incredulous look; and then he slipped the bandage down from Flower's eyes. "A sackful, you said."

"We've got to count up and see how much there is, Walter.

We'll need you to help."

It took them more than an hour and a half to make even a hurried, rough calculation. Every letter had to be opened, and the sum inside noted for sending letters of thanks. Then all had to be quickly added up; and the time was ticking toward noon in a way that made Tess's heart jump. The total was £94 7s. And the time was 11.45.

"God bless us all, let's take it to the boss quick!" said Walter.

*In the farmyard they threw themselves out as the van came to a stop and raced across the concrete to the stable.*

"It's enough for buying the horses and paying their fare", said John, as they hurried to the farmhouse. "And with our own fund added, we'll be able to send quite a lot to the horses home, too, toward their keep."

And that, exciting though it was, was not quite the end. One day the next fall, when Walter was visiting his horses, the manager of the horses' home said to him: "I suppose you know that the County Plowing Match is being held in this village? Why not come over and enter Flower and Captain, just once more?"

And Walter did just that.

Tess and John still have the letter he wrote to them afterwards, which says: "I only wish you could have been there and seen my horses get their dozen and century! I reckon you'd have been as proud as I was, since, we'd never have done it without you."

*"I only wish you could have been there and seen my horses get their dozen and century! I reckon you'd have been as proud as I was, since, we'd never have done it without you."*

# DRAFT HORSES

Flower and Captain are among the last in a great tradition of heavy working horses. Until the invention of the steam engine in the 1800s, the horse was the chief means of transportation and of work on the farm. Today, tractors have taken the place of horses, though teams can still be seen at country fairs.

**City life**
For most of the 19th century, public transportation in the cities was provided by horse-drawn omnibuses. The work was so hard that a horse's working life was only four years.

**Plowing the fields**
Before the invention of the tractor, farming depended on horses for plowing the fields, and pulling hay carts and wagons. Most farm machinery could be pulled by a team of two horses, like Flower and Captain. In the US, though, huge combine harvesters were pulled by teams of 40 horses.

*Some breweries still use horse-drawn carts today.*

*For shows, the mane is plaited and decorated with ribbons to show the strong neck.*

**In industry**
Draft horses were used in all forms of industry. They moved heavy machines, pulled coal wagons, even pulled the early trains.

**Showing off**
Although heavy horse breeds no longer play a significant role in farming, their strength and dignity still grace many shows.

*The long hair around the feet is called feather.*

# POST TIME

from *The Black Stallion and the Girl* by Walter Farley

*Few writers have managed to convey the breathless thrills of horse racing more vividly than Walter Farley. In this extract from his* Black Stallion *series of novels, the Black, with Alec on board, is attempting to win the $50,000 Roseben handicap. It's a close-run thing...*

At Aqueduct the following Saturday, the Black was saddled for the feature race on the afternoon program. Stripped of all useless fat and flesh, he was in his finest shape.

He seemed to know he had never looked so handsome, for he feigned impatience and rebellion against Alec, who stood at his head. The Black pawed the ground and half-reared. His mane, so carefully brushed and combed only moments before, fell tousled around his head and neck. The pure curve of his high, crested neck arched majestically, and his great eyes flashed fire as he surveyed the other horses in the saddling paddock.

"Hold him still, won't you?" Henry Dailey said, tightening the girth strap. His voice was gruff, as if speaking to an employee instead of to Alec. Henry's forehead was so deeply wrinkled that his eyebrows were separated from his gray hair only by a thin line of skin.

When the old man had the girth as he wanted it, he straightened and placed a hand on the lead pad beneath the saddle.

"No horse should carry so much weight, but we'll show 'em. We're dodging nobody."

Alec said not a word, knowing nothing was expected of him. Henry was talking for his own benefit. The heavy weights that track handicappers were assigning to the Black in every race he entered must eventually set a turf record. They created a lot of tension before a race,

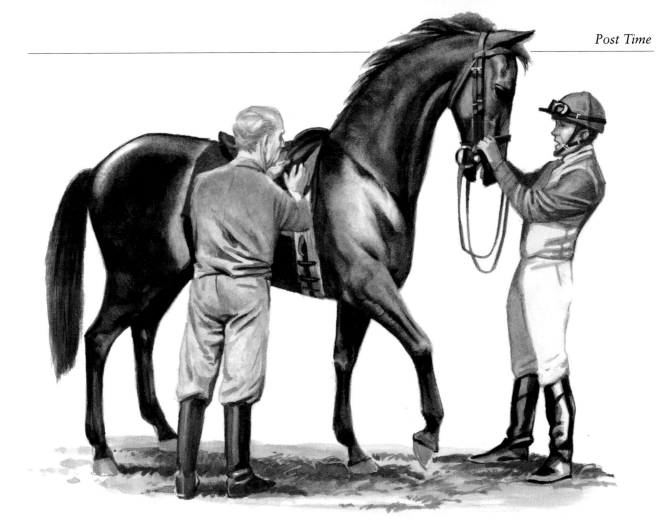

*When the old man had the girth as he wanted it, he straightened and placed a hand on the lead pad beneath the saddle.*

so Alec understood and tolerated his old friend's gruffness.

The weights were assigned in order to give every horse in a race a chance at top money. The amount each horse carried on his back was made by taking into consideration his race record, his workouts, and his physical condition. Lead weights inserted in a pad beneath the saddle were added, when necessary, to the weight of the rider in order to meet the track handicapper's assigned weight. Champions carried the highest weights of all, and the Black was consistently carrying more weight than any other horse in racing.

Henry stepped back, a stocky man with a barrel-shaped chest. His eyes, like his mouth, were narrow slits in a round-cheeked face. His nose was his only prominent feature, being hooked, almost like the beak of a bird of prey. He examined the stallions's hocks and forelegs, the solidity

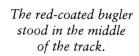

of his flanks and chest, looking for any sign of soreness or weakness.

The paddock judge called, "Riders, mount your horses, please!"

Alec was boosted into the saddle and, picking up the reins, he spoke quietly to the Black. Once Alec was up, the stallion usually settled down, his nervousness being quickly replaced by an eagerness to get on with the business of racing. The Black didn't like to wait.

"Any instructions?" Alec asked Henry. The trainer had mounted Napoleon, their stable pony, and was accompanying them to the post.

Henry shook his head. "Just ride your race," he said, grabbing the Black's bridle. "There's nothing I can tell you that you don't already know." He moved Napoleon's hindquarters between the Black and a horse following too closely behind.

*The red-coated bugler stood in the middle of the track.*

The red-coated bugler, wearing shiny black boots and a black hunting cap, stood in the middle of the track, with a long coach horn pressed to his lips. Henry shivered with anticipation at the sound of the call to the post. He had lost count of how many years ago it was that he had heard it for the first time. He was as old and gray and sway-backed as the gelding he rode, and just as fat. But each of them still had a job to do.

The great stands were packed and overflowing. Everybody was tense. Everybody was waiting. There were nine horses in the post parade for the Roseben Handicap, a distance of seven furlongs (seven-eighths of a mile) for a purse of $50,000. But the crowd saw only one entry, the Black.

Everybody knew the champion would not be found lacking speed, but there was always racing luck to consider... plus the heavy burden of 138 pounds on his back against light-weighted horses, some carrying only 103 pounds. Besides, it was a short race for the Black. He might have trouble catching the others before the finish if his rider made a single mistake.

There would be bumping and swerving in so large a field. So this might be a day to remember, the day the greatest handicap runner of all time was beaten, and they would have been there to see it!

Alec wrapped the reins about his hands. At the starting gate Henry left him. Between the Black's ears Alec could see the sun dropping behind the New York City skyscrapers to the west. He glanced at the other horses and had no fear of them. It was only their riders who could beat him. They were among the best in the business and capable of taking quick advantage of any mistake he might make, even helping him to make a big one that would cost the Black a victory.

They were on either side of him, milling behind the gate, awaiting assistant starters to lead their mounts into the padded, narrow stalls.

*He glanced at the other horses and had no fear of them. It was only their riders who could beat him.*

Each rode slowly, whip in hand and ready. Their faces disclosed no emotion. They all might have been carved of wood or cut from toughest leather. Their bodies were hard and fit beneath glossy silks; lips were thin and tightly clasped, looking cruel, as did their narrowed eyes.

"Get down to business," Alec cautioned himself. A moment later he rode the Black into the Number 1 stall. The other riders followed him into the gate, their voices rising above the din, hard and arrogant, shouting at each other and to the starter. All of them had supreme confidence in their ability to wring every last ounce of speed out of their mounts by the use of massive wrists and broad, thick hands. Slim, all muscle and bone, they sat on their racing machines and waited.

The bell clanged and the stall doors flew open! Instinctively, Alec let

*The bell clanged and the stall doors flew open!*
*Instinctively, Alec let the reins slide through his hands.*

the reins slide through his hands, his voice joining the cries of the other riders, "Yah! Yah! Yah!"

His hands suddenly tightened on the reins again, squeezing rather than pulling, as a horse moved directly in front of them and stayed there. Alec looked for racing room, knowing he'd been caught unprepared. He tried every trick he knew to get the Black free of the rush of bodies on every side of him.

His whip came down, not touching the Black, in an attempt to scare off the packed horses and riders. The wind carried his shouts to the other jockeys, his words threatening and challenging, those of a rider fighting for racing room and, perhaps, his very life. He drove his heels into the Black's sides and his hands went forward in brutal suddenness, urging the horse forward with all his strength.

They raced down the long backstretch chute.

There were three furlongs to go to the far turn, two furlongs around the bend, and two more furlongs for home. He had to get the Black free and running before they reached the turn, for the stallion's long strides made it difficult to negotiate turns and he was apt to run out, losing ground. There might not be enough distance left in the stretch run to overtake the leaders.

Alec looked for a clear way through the traffic jam. He let the Black out another notch, not truly knowing where he was going anyway, for his need to do something was very great. He felt not only anger with himself but guilt. He sought relief in speed and more speed, and danger as well.

He had made a mistake, but there was time to correct it. He leaned into the Black, taking him over to the rail, only to pull him up abruptly when the opening he had spotted was closed by a plunging horse. Alec took the stallion back, moving toward the middle of the pack, inches away from the heaving hindquarters of horses directly ahead.

*The Black was fighting for his head, trying to run over the horses in front of him.*

The Black was fighting for his head, trying to run over the horses in front of him. Beyond the bunched field, two horses were free and clear. Light-weighted sprinters, their legs moved in short, pistonlike strides, taking them toward the far turn like small, wound up whirlwinds. Alec knew he had to catch them soon or the Black would be beaten.

He tried to move the stallion between two outside horses, but was shut off again. He had to bring the Black almost to a stop to avoid going down; his hands took a tight hold on the reins and he jerked hard. The force of it wrenched the bit in the stallion's mouth, tearing the flesh at the corners.

He heard the Black scream in rage and pain, and his heart felt a deep anguish. Yet he'd no alternative if he wanted to avoid serious injury … even death. Suddenly he saw an opening and launched the Black forward again.

Lathered foam whipped from the stallion's neck as he shot between horses. None of the jockeys had expected such a rush from behind with so little room between them. Above the din of racing hoofs, Alec heard the challenges the other riders hurled at him. One false step and the Black would go down. He guided him through the mass of horseflesh in a single rush, avoiding hoofs and bodies by inches. He rode as he never had before, using all his wits and skill with a strength and harshness he had not known he possessed. His daring, combined with the Black's fury and speed, astonished the others and threw them off balance. They separated, and the leaping black stallion sped between them, free and clear!

Leaving the pack behind, Alec took the Black into the turn with only the two front-running sprinters ahead. They were setting a dizzy pace. Did he still have the time and distance to catch them? The Black devoured the track with his long strides, yet ran wide going around the turn. Alec tried to guide him over to the rail, but his extreme speed made it impossible. The leaders were already leaving the turn and entering the home stretch with just two furlongs to go.

Alec flattened himself against the stallion's neck, his face buried in the mane. There was no need to urge the Black on, for the racing stallion knew what was expected of him. He came off the turn, stretched low to the ground in the fury of his run. He was catching the leaders fast, outrunning them with every magnificent stride.

The crowd was on its feet. Was this to the be the day the Black lost for the first time? The two leaders flashed by the sixteenth pole, their strides coming as one, a closely matched team of two, fighting, clawing their way to the finish line.

The Black came down the track with a swiftness that could not be denied. But the fans were not really aware of the awesome power of his body, for he ran with such ease that his strides seemed to be a single flowing movement.

The finish line was far enough away for Alec to know that the distance had not run out on them. He shouted into the wind created by his horse. Only the Black heard his cry of victory, but he was the only one that mattered. He caught the leaders two strides from the wire and swept under it all by himself.

*... he ran with such ease that his strides seemed to be a single flowing movement.*

# FLAT RACING

The Black is a champion flat-racing horse. This form of racing, where horses race on a course without jumps, is the fastest type of race. As described in the story, the sport is full of excitement and tension both for the horses and jockeys taking part, and the huge number of spectators who pack the stands.

**Royal patron**
Racing is known as "the sport of kings" because of its long association with the British monarchy. King Henry VIII was the first royal patron of horse racing.

*Alec and the Black's race is a short distance of 7/8ths of a mile. Most flat races are over a mile long. Horses may reach speeds of 40 miles per hour (65 km an hour).*

**Weighty matters**
Champion racehorses, like the Black, carry lead weights in the saddle, added to the weight of the jockey as a handicap. The combined weight of the jockey and saddle is checked before and after a race.

**Thoroughbred**
Thoroughbred horses are used in all forms of horse racing. They have been bred over the last 200 years for their speed, courage, strength, and stamina.

**Flat out**
British jockeys take their racehorses out for early morning training gallops every day of the year, whatever the weather. They train hard for the 16 national flat races held in the UK between March and October.

# MY FRIEND FLICKA

from the novel by Mary O'Hara

*Flicka, an unbroken, part-mustang filly belongs to a boy named Ken who lives on a ranch in Wyoming. She is ill with fever, brought on by infected wounds, and rapidly wasting away. Ken's father believes Flicka is sure to die. He wants Gus, one of his ranch hands, to put her out of her misery; but Ken is determined to cure his beloved pony.*

After supper, Ken carried Flicka her oats, but she would hardly touch them. She stood with her head hanging; but when he stroked it and talked to her, she pressed her face into his chest and was content.

He could feel the burning heat of her body. It didn't seem possible that anything so thin could be alive.

Soon Ken saw Gus coming into the pasture carrying the Winchester. When he saw Ken, he changed his direction and walked along as if he was out to shoot cottontails.

Ken ran to him, "When are you going to do it, Gus?"

"Ay was goin' down soon now, before it got dark –"

"Gus, don't do it tonight. Wait till morning. Just one more night, Gus."

"Vell, in de morning den, but it got to be done, Ken. Yer fadder gives de order."

"I know. I won't say anything more."

Gus went back to the bunkhouse and Ken returned to Flicka.

He stood by her, smoothing and caressing her as he always did. Usually he talked to her, but he couldn't do that now. There was only one thing on his mind, and he couldn't talk about that. Now and then, as if it came from someone else, he heard a little moan. It was he himself that was moaning.

Below the cottonwood trees, the darkness fell swiftly, and Ken and Flicka were hidden in it together. It folded around them and held them close. He couldn't see her, and she couldn't see him; but he moved around her, and her head turned to follow him so that her muzzle rested against him, as she always did. The darkness pressed them closer together.

At nine o'clock, Howard [a ranch hand] was sent by Nell [Ken's mother] to call Ken. He stood at the corral gate, shouting.

Again there was the sound of soft moaning. Then Ken pressed a last kiss

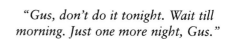

*"Gus, don't do it tonight. Wait till morning. Just one more night, Gus."*

on Flicka's face, and went up the hill under the cottonwoods.

Flicka was still standing in her nursery when the full moon rose at ten. It was the hunter's moon, as yellow as the harvest moon, but not so large.

The night was silent, with the profound silence of a calm sea. Even the faint roaring of the earth, like the roaring in a shell, was hushed. It waited.

If the mind of a living being – man or beast – is clear, there are forewarnings of the approach of death. The body gets ready. One by one the active functions cease, till, at last, the currents of living force become inverted in a downward spiral into which the creature is drawn, spinning faster and faster toward the vortex.

*Though, from force of habit, she stood by the feed box, she had not touched the oats.*

All of this can be felt; and, feeling this, Flicka knew that her time had come.

Her head hung low. Her legs were slightly splayed under her. Though, from force of habit, she stood by the feed box, she had not touched the oats. Every cell in her body was seared with fierce, burning fever. Sometimes her mind was in a drifting delirium, sometimes in coma, sometimes clear and knowing.

Flicka's wounds did not pain her, but the suction of the downward spiral was an agony felt through every part of her. Now and then her young body found strength to fight against it. She struggled and lifted her head. She turned toward the path down which Ken's running feet had come a thousand times that summer. He was all she had, and all she could hope for. But tonight there was no sound, no step, no help.

For minutes she stayed this way, her ears strained for the sound of him, longing and listening. Then she gradually succumbed to the tug of those inner quicksands, and drooped, wavering, over the earth.

In one of the surges of rebellion, she neighed.

Miles away on the upland, her sire, Banner, heard and answered. And the loud kingly cry, made into a faint trumpet call by the distance, drifted across the miles, across the roads, across the barbed wire barricades that intervened, and burned hope into the fever that was consuming Flicka.

She began to prance jerkily, like a marionette pulled by strings. All that was left in her of will and power gathered itself and she trotted downstream along the bank.

She jarred to a sudden stop, standing in terror with head low and feet braced out as if she had come face to face with a phantom. Gradually the terror went out of her, but she held the ridiculous posture as if unable to move. Her head turned again to the ranch house ... *would he come?*

She was thirsty. The smell of the fresh running water drew her. She waded into the stream and drank. When she got her fill, and lifted her head she turned it again to the house. The cool water rippled against her legs.

There was no sound from the house, no feet running upon the path, and suddenly the last of her strength was gone. Lunging forward, she fell, half on the bank, half in the water, and lay there struggling convulsively.

At last she was still.

Some minutes later, from ten miles away on the towering black-timbered shoulders of Pole Mountain, there stole out the most desolate cry in all the world – the howl of the gray timber wolf. It rode on the upper air without a tremor, high and thin, pointed as a needle.

Ken had seen the hunter's moon rise over the eastern horizon before he went upstairs. He hadn't completely undressed, but he had the sheet drawn up to his chin in case his mother or father come in to look at him. He heard them talking together in their room as they undressed.

*She was thirsty. The smell of the fresh running water drew her.*

They took a long time. It seemed hours to him hours before the whole house was quiet – as quiet as the night was outside.

He heard Flicka neigh, but he didn't hear Banner answer. Human ears were not keen enough to catch that distant greeting. He knew Flicka was neighing for him. He heard the wolf howl.

He waited another hour, till everyone was so deep asleep there would be no chance of their hearing. Then he stole out of bed and put on the rest of his clothes.

He carried his shoes and crept down the hall, past the door of his parents' room, taking half a minute a step.

On the far end of the terrace, he sat down and put on his shoes, his heart pounding and the blood almost suffocating him.

He kept whispering, "I'm coming, Flicka – I'm coming."

His feet pattered down the path. He ran as fast as he could.

It was so dark under the cottonwood trees that he had to stand for a moment, getting used to the darkness, before he could be sure that Flicka was not there. There stood her feed box – but the filly was gone.

He ran wildly here and there. At last, when there was no sign of her, he began a systematic search through the pasture. He dared not call aloud, but he whispered – "Flicka – oh, Flicka – where are you?"

At last he found her down the creek lying in the water. Her head had been on the bank; but as she lay there, the current of the stream had sucked and pulled at her. She had had no strength to resist, and little by little her head had slipped down until, when Ken got there, only the muzzle was resting on the bank. The body and legs were swinging in the stream.

Ken slid into the water, sitting on the bank, and he hauled at her head. But she was heavy, and the current dragged like a weight. He began to sob because he had no strength to draw her out.

Then he found leverage for his heels against some rocks in the bed of the stream, and he braced himself against them. He pulled with all his might, and her head came up on to his knees. He held it cradled in his arms.

He was glad she had died of her own accord, in the cool water, under the moon, instead of being shot by Gus. Then, putting his face close to hers, and looking searchingly into her eyes, he saw that she was alive and looking back at him.

The long night passed.

The moon slowly slid across the heavens.

The water rippled over Ken's legs, and over Flicka's body. Gradually the heat and the fever went out of her, and the cool running water washed and washed her wounds.

That night took a heavy toll from Ken; but for Flicka there was resurgence. At the moment when Ken drew her into his arms and cried her name, the spell of the downward spiral was broken; Flicka was released and not once again did she feel it. The life

*Ken slid into the water, sitting on the bank, and he hauled at her head. But she was heavy, and the current dragged like a weight*

currents in her body turned, and in weak and wavering fashion, flowed upward. A power went into her from Ken; all his youth and strength and magnetism given to her freely and abundantly on the stream of his love – from his ardent eyes to hers.

But for Ken, there was the creeping numbness of those parts where the head and neck of the filly pressed. Then the deep chill from the cold water running over his legs, his thighs, almost up to his waist. Long before the night was over, his teeth were chattering and his body shaking with chills.

It didn't matter. Nothing mattered except holding Flicka, and holding the life in her.

*At the moment when Ken drew her into his arms and cried*
*her name, the spell of the downward spiral was broken;*
*Flicka was released and not once again did she feel it.*

# BASIC HORSE CARE

The horse is the biggest and most easily injured of all the domesticated animals. Looking after one and making sure it stays healthy takes up a lot of time and is a big responsibility. But with the right care, good exercise, and proper feeding you will have a loyal and trusty animal who may live to be over 30 years old.

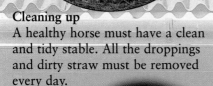

**Cleaning up**
A healthy horse must have a clean and tidy stable. All the droppings and dirty straw must be removed every day.

**Regular exercise**
To keep healthy, horses kept in a stable should be taken out for exercise at least two hours a day. If you don't have time to ride your horse, it can be exercised on a lungeing rein for 20 minutes instead.

*A horse that is unwell should be kept in a stable for box rest and not ridden.*

**Balanced diet**
Feeding your horse a good diet will help keep it healthy. Horses have small stomachs, so they need to eat small amounts often. Hay and fresh drinking water provide enough basic nutrition. Ready-mixed cereals provide extra vitamins and minerals.

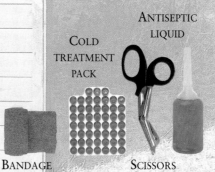

ANTISEPTIC LIQUID

COLD TREATMENT PACK

BANDAGE

SCISSORS

**First aid kit**
A basic first aid kit is essential to treat any minor injuries or wounds. A vet should be called to treat any serious illness or injury.

# JILL'S GYMKHANA

from the novel by Ruby Ferguson

*Jill had always dreamed of having her own pony. After
overcoming many trials and tribulations, she manages to buy
Danny Boy, learn to ride, and enter Chatton Show. This extract
comes from the first in a highly popular series of novels.*

"What lovely jumps," said Ann.
"They look like precipices to me," I remarked. "But they are
lovely, just the same."

We were leaning over the railings to watch the first event after the
interval, which was the Open Jumping. I always think this event is the
most wonderful thing in the world to watch; there is something utterly
splendid about it, to see the tall magnificent horses soar into the air under
their skillful riders' touch, all in such harmony and effortless control.
Everything around is beautiful, too – the white painted jumps and the
bright green field, the eager faces around the ring, and the grandstand
packed with people ready to cheer. And to think that there are actually
people who never go to gymkhanas! It makes me think of those noble
lines of the poet:

"Breathes there the man with soul so dead,

Who never to himself hath said,

'I will arise and go to a gymkhana?'"

When number thirty-three was called we saw Mrs. Darcy ride into
the ring on a lovely lean gray called Martha, who I knew from my own
experience was capable of anything if she could keep her temperament in
control. This was one of Martha's good days, and she jumped a
beautifully collected round, finishing with only one and a half faults.

"I think she's got a chance," I said excitedly.

However, a strange man on a black hunter won first place with no faults. And a boy of twenty, who we were told had won Firsts all over the country, was second with one fault. To my joy, Mrs. Darcy got third place, which was pretty good considering the competition; there were nineteen entries.

With open event over, the stewards began to lower the jumps for the novice jumping. In this event, I had the thrill of seeing my friend Angela jump a clear round on Inez, and everybody cheered like crazy. In the end she tied for first place with a hunting man called Markham, who kept a lot of horses. They had a tie-breaker and Angela won! It was a great

*We were leaning over the railings to watch*
*the first event after the interval, which*
*was the Open Jumping.*

*Ann and I rode round to the collecting ring, and we both had the feeling that our hearts were jumping about inside and doing gymkhanas on their own.*

honor to have won a first in the novice jumping at Chatton Show.

Then the jumps were lowered again and this time it was our turn. Ann and I rode round to the collecting ring, and we both had the feeling that our hearts were jumping about inside and doing gymkhanas on their own. In any case they say that if you don't have this feeling you are not very good.

There were twenty-six children competing, of all ages from twelve to sixteen. And there was the famous Maureen Chase looking cool and distant, and the famous Frank Stabley who I thought looked an awfully nice boy, and Susan Pyke, backing her pink horse into the others and getting black looks from everybody.

She kept saying, "I can't help it. He's so full of spirit. You see – he's a show jumper, not just an ordinary pony," – and she gave all our "ordinary" ponies very scornful glances.

"Well, you're up," said Ann to Susan, as a boy called Peters came riding back to the ring and the megaphone called out "thirteen faults." "So you can let your charger charge!"

All eyes were on Susan as she made a spectacular entrance; but I didn't like the way the roan pawed the ground, or the look in his eye. He had a silly, wild look, not the sensible clever look of a pony who is going to do any good at jumping.

He went straight at the first jump, which was the bush, before Susan was ready, and nearly threw her. But he cleared the jump with inches to spare; and a girl next to me said, "Some show jumper!"

Susan was now trying to collect her pony, but he refused to be collected. He went full tilt at the next jump, which was the gate. He soared into the air, bucked in mid-air, got his feet in a knot, and sent Susan flying six yards. She landed with a thud. The pink horse, having done his stuff, ran right out of the ring, neighing at the top of his voice.

Susan sat there on the ground, quite openly weeping for all to see. Two stewards went and helped her up, and there was obviously nothing the matter with her. She soon returned back among us looking very low indeed.

"Serves her right!" said a girl next to me. "She always ruins every gymkhana for everybody else. They ought to disqualify her permanently."

Susan could not help hearing this remark; and Ann, who was soft-hearted, went across to her and said kindly, "It was just tough luck, Susan."

*Susan sat there on the ground,*
*quite openly weeping for all to see.*

"Oh, thank you, Ann," said Susan, in a very humble and heartfelt tone, quite different from her usual bragging one.

Meanwhile Maureen Chase had gone in and done an efficient but uninspiring round, to finish up with two faults. And a boy called Michael Grant was making the crowd roar by sending everything flying.

Then it was Ann's turn, and I knew she would enjoy herself because she didn't expect much from Seraphine. To my surprise – and hers – Seraphine jumped the round of her life, finishing with only four faults. She and Ann looked so pretty and graceful jumping that the crowd clapped and cheered like crazy. The judges all smiled with pleasure at Ann as she rode so neatly and nicely off.

Frank Stabley had very bad luck. He took four jumps perfectly; but just as he approached the triple bar, a dog fight broke out in the crowd only about five yards away. Frank's pony reared, and then being quite upset gave him three refusals. I was awfully sorry about this as Frank certainly was an excellent jumper.

Then my number was called. As I rode into the ring I had the strangest feeling of being really happy; and I could tell that Danny Boy was feeling the same way. I whispered into his ear, "Now angel, don't bother about all those people. We're just jumping for fun, like we do at home, and it's going to be great."

He arched his neck, and looked both proud and serious, and so at a collected canter we approached the first jump. I only had to whisper, "Hup!" and the next second we were over, so smoothly that I had hardly felt him ride. I knew then that he was going to do it! I knew that he and I were just like one single person. So we took the gate, and then the wall, and then – with only the slightest pause – the tricky in-and-out. We were coming up to the triple bar now. I stroked his neck and whispered, "Don't rush, boy. Do just as I tell you." I had forgotten the crowd and everything except those three white bars ahead, sparkling in the sunshine. "Now!" I said suddenly. "Hup!"

And then I did feel him soar. I felt him gather his legs up in that lovely careful way of his, and I felt the rush of the wind on my face. Then I could hardly believe it for we were on the ground again and everybody was clapping, and I wasn't quite conscious as I patted him and couldn't say a word as he carried me out of the ring and the megaphones blared, "Clear round."

*And then I did feel him soar. I felt him gather his legs up in that lovely careful way of his.*

Was this really me, or was I dreaming? Surely jumping a clear round in the under-sixteens at Chatton Show was the sort of thing that could only happen in a dream? But I came around when some of my friends began to thump me on the back until my tie nearly flew off. I gasped, "Well, it's nothing really. About six other people are sure to jump clear rounds."

But strangely enough nobody else did, and soon three of us were called in. I was first, a boy called Lloyd was second with one fault, and Maureen Chase was third with two. After I had received my red rosette, I was told that I must also go up to the grandstand to receive the Hopley Challenge Cup, to be held for a year. So with a scarlet face and dummy hands I took this large silver cup in my arms. I muttered something like "Oh, thanks!" to somebody who I afterward found out was Lord Hopley. And then my at-no-times-particularly-graceful exit was completely ruined when I dropped the black ebony base of the thing, which fell on the ground with a resounding thud and had to be rescued by a steward, while resounding howls of derision mingled with the cheers of the crowd.

One place where I simply couldn't look was the front row of the stand where Mom and my friends were sitting. I let myself go in the usual wild gallop around the ring; and when I came to the exit, there they all were.

"Good job," was all that Martin said. And Mom added, "Not bad at all, Jill. But why on earth did you have to drop that thing?"

"There's nothing left now but the Grand parade," said Martin. "Hand Danny Boy over to Bob here, who'll give him a rubdown. You scoot off and get cleaned up."

"OK," I said. "I'll want your powder, Mom."

So with my cap, boots, and jodhpurs brushed, my tie retied, and my face sophisticatedly powdered, I rejoined Danny Boy, who under Bob's skillful hand looked as if he was made of patent leather. Then, headed by the local band, we joined in the Grand parade – in which everything that has won firsts in the show marches slowly around and around the ring.

Danny Boy gave me quite a look when he found he had to do a collected walk behind a lot of fat cows.

At last it was all over. As I rode out I passed Frank Stabley and his father, and they smiled at me. I heard Frank say, "Look, Dad, that's the girl who won. Pretty good, eh?"

And Mr. Stabley said, "They say that Martin Lowe trained her, so you'd expect something."

*After I had received my red rosette, I was told that I must also go up to the grandstand to receive the Hopley Challenge Cup, to be held for a year.*

I was really happy. But I didn't feel the least bit cocky or conceited, because I knew that I'd had a lot of luck and that this was the sort of day which only comes to a person once in a lifetime.

As we all left the showground together, Mrs. Darcy and gave me a happy salute.

"Well, well well!" she said, in her loud, hearty way. "It certainly has been Jill's gymkhana!"

And with those magic words ringing in my ears, I turned my pony happily toward home.

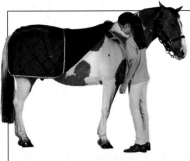

**Grooming**
Careful grooming is needed before a show to make a pony's coat, mane, and tail shine and look as beautiful as possible.

# SHOW TIME!

Jill takes part in a show-jumping class; but there are also dressage, showing classes, and gymkhana games among the events at horse shows. However big or small the show, a lot of hard work is needed both before and on the day itself. But whether you win a prize or not, a show is sure to provide a fun and exciting day out for you and your pony.

**Getting to the show**
If a pony needs to be transported to a show in a trailer, it is important to arrive in plenty of time. A pony will need time to get used to his new surroundings.

**Gymkhana games**
As well as being fun, gymkhana games test a rider's balance and skill. Here, the rider has to lean over to pick up a bottle before racing back to the start of the course. The winner is the one who completes the task in the fastest time.

**Show jumping**
Jill wins her show-jumping event because Danny Boy gets a clear round — he jumps over the course of fences without knocking any of the poles off.

**Prize winner**
Jill describes what a wonderful feeling it is to win a prize. But it's a team effort and it's important to thank a pony, too.

# THE FIRST MAN ON MANCHA'S BACK

from *The Tale of Two Horses* by A.F. Tschiffely

*In the 1930s, A. F. Tschiffely made an epic two and a half year journey from Argentina to Washington on his wild Criollo horses, Gato and Mancha. Here is Mancha's account of his breaking in cowboy fashion, a quick and frightening experience.*

One morning several cowboys came toward the corral; and as we nervously watched, we noticed that our master was among them.

Before I realized what all these men had come for, I was lassoed and pulled out of the corral. My legs were then tied in such a way that it was impossible for me to move or kick without falling. I was so frightened that I wasn't aware that a man strapped one of those strange things, called saddles, on my back. Almost at the same instant the ropes with which my legs were bound were untied and taken off.

At first I thought the thing on my back was a puma or some other wild animal, so I arched my back, and put my head between my forelegs, and bucked for all I was worth. I fought with terror and fury and tried every trick I knew to throw enemies off my back.

Only wild horses know how to buck properly; for if an enemy leaps on them they must do this to shake it off and thus save their lives. Pumas and tigers usually jump on their victims' backs and bite their necks to kill them. To throw them off, we put our heads between our forelegs and arch our backs – like cats do when they see a dog – and then we buck as hard as we can.

I fought so furiously that I raised a cloud of dust. But every time

I bucked I heard a loud "hee-hoo!" Soon I found out that it was not a puma, but a cowboy who was sitting on my back. I also noticed that the other men were watching and waving their hats. Realizing that I simply couldn't shake off the man by bucking, I thought I'd try

*I arched my back, and put my head between my forelegs, and bucked for all I was worth.*

to flee; so I raced over the prairie. Every now and then I stopped suddenly, but even this didn't move the man whose whip and spurs urged me on, faster and faster.

Seeing a tree, I decided to race toward it and brush off the rider. But before I had gone far, two cowboys on horses came alongside me and pushed me in the other direction. After a while I was so tired and out of breath that I simply couldn't run and buck any more; so I stood still, trembling all over. I had lost the fight. The gaucho was still on my back. What a man! How he could ride!

When I had been guided back to the corral, the saddle was taken off me and placed on Gato, whose resistance was also in vain.

Although I was dripping with perspiration and shaking all over with exhaustion, I watched what was happening to my pal outside.

He fought so bravely that all our friends in the wilds would have been very proud of him. But again the man proved to be a good rider – and poor Gato also lost his fight. Puffing and panting and with flecks of foam all over him, he was brought back into the corral. When the cowboys had gone, and we had cooled off a little, the two of us had a long talk about our latest experience with men.

For a few days after this we were saddled and ridden. We soon realized that our riders intended us no harm; and as it was no use struggling against them, we slowly gave in. Once or twice we managed to throw off the rider, but he always fell on his feet like a cat. And before we had time to run away he was on our backs again.

Very soon we gave up bucking, and, instead, trotted or cantered in whatever direction our riders guided us.

When we were not being ridden we were kept in the corral; and we began to wonder if we would ever be let out again to join our pals who were happily grazing outside in the big field.

Somehow we felt that something was to happen soon, and as the days passed we felt this more and more.

# BRONCO BUSTING

"What a man! How he could ride!" Mancha exclaims after unsuccessfully trying to throw off the cowboy that is his first experience of a man sitting on his back. Cowboy skills in riding unbroken horses – known as bronco busting – were developed in the early days of cattle-ranching. Today these skills can most easily be seen at rodeos.

**Bronco riding**
Saddle-bronc riding is the most difficult of the rodeo events. The rider has to stay on a bucking horse for eight seconds, with only a single rope to hold on to. The horses are often bred specifically for the rodeo and are no longer wild.

**Calf-roping**
In this rodeo event, the skills of horse and rider are equally tested. The rider must first lasso a calf with his rope. Next he must get off his horse and tie the calf's legs in the fastest possible time while the horse holds the rope tight. Speed and agility are the most valued qualities in the horse.

*A bucking bronco arches its back and puts its head between its forelegs.*

**Criollo horses**
Tschiffely knew what he was doing when he tamed Mancha and Gato and chose to ride them on his great journey. The Criollo is a very tough breed of horse and one of the most enduring. They are known for their ability to carry heavy weights over long distances.

*As Mancha explains, wild horses buck because they fear an enemy on their back.*

**Western saddle**
This saddle is specially designed for the cowboy. The high cantle at the back stops the cowboy from slipping out of the saddle backward. The horn at the front is used for tying a rope.

# ACKNOWLEDGMENTS

The publishers would like to thank the copyright holders for permission
to reproduce the following copyright material:
**Monica Edwards**: for "The Champions". Copyright © The Estate of Monica Edwards. Reprinted by
permission of Barlows on behalf of the Estate. **Walter Farley**: for the extract from *The Black Stallion
and the Girl*. Copyright © 1971 by Walter Farley. Reprinted by permission of Random House Inc.
**Ruby Ferguson**: for the extract from *Jill's Gymkhana*, published by Hodder and Stoughton Ltd.
Copyright © Ruby Ferguson 1949. Reproduced by permission of Hodder and Stoughton Ltd.
**Marguerite Henry**: for the extract from *Misty of Chincoteague*. Copyright © 1947 and copyright
renewed © 1975 Marguerite Henry. Reprinted with the permission of Simon & Schuster Books for
Young Readers, an imprint of Simon & Schuster Children's Publishing Division. **Roger Lancelyn Green**:
for "Pegasus", originally published by G. Bell & Sons Ltd as "The Prince and the Flying Horse", from
*Old Greek Fairy Stories* (1958). Copyright © Richard Lancelyn Green. Reprinted with permission of
the Literary Estate of Roger Lancelyn Green. **Elyne Mitchell**: for the extract from *The Silver Brumby*,
published by HarperCollins Australia. Copyright © Elyne Mitchell 1958. Reprinted by permission of
Curtis Brown (Aust) Pty Ltd., Sydney. **Mary O'Hara**: for the extract from *My Friend Flicka*, published
by Egmont Children's Books. Copyright © Mary O'Hara 1941. Reprinted by permission of Laurence
Pollinger Limited and the Estate of Mary O'Hara. **Diana Pullein-Thompson**: Jennifer Luithlen Agency
for an extract from *A Foal for Candy* by Diana Pullein-Thompson, published by Hutchinson.
Copyright © 1981 Diana Pullein-Thompson. **A.F. Tschiffely**: for the extract from *The Tale of Two
Horses*. John Johnson Ltd on behalf of the Estate. Copyright © The Estate of A. F. Tschiffely 1934.
Every effort has been made to obtain permission to reproduce copyright material but there
may be cases where we have been unable to trace a copyright holder. Dorling Kindersley
will be happy to correct any omissions in future printings.

Further photography by: Geoff Brightling, Peter Chadwick, Gordon Clayton,
Andy Crawford, Bob Langrish, Tim Ridley, Karl Shone, Jerry Young,

t = top, b = bottom, c = centre, l = left, r = right, a = above, bgr = background.

AKG London Ltd: 31bgr, tl; Art & Ancient Architecture: 31cr;
Bridgeman Art Library: 15tl, 31clb; Christie's Images: 63bgr;
Mary Evans Picture Library: 25tr, 47bgr, 63cl; Kit Houghton: 7tr,
25c, br, 47bl; Bob Langrish: 15bgr, 31bl, 41tl, 63bl, br, 73bgr, tr,
br, c, 91bgr, cl, c, 95c; Peter Newark's Americana: 95br; Frank
Spooner Pictures: 95bgr, tr; Tony Stone Images: 15bl; 25bgr, cl, bl.

EASY FOIL Recipes

Publications International, Ltd.
Favorite Brand Name Recipes at www.fbnr.com

Photography on pages 15, 19, 27, 31, 41, 45, 49, 65, 81, 83, 85 and 87 by Peter Dean Ross Photographs.

Recipe development on pages 14, 16, 26, 33, 48, 64 and 70 by Susan Garard.
Recipe development on pages 18, 32, 38 and 40 by Gregg Hollander.
Recipe development on pages 30, 44, 47, 80, 88 and 90 by Nancy Ross Ryan.
Recipe development on pages 39, 84, 86 and 89 by Karen Straus.

**Pictured on the front cover** *(clockwise from top left):* Sweet & Sour Chicken *(page 64),* Baked Cinnamon Apple *(page 80),* Spicy Pistachio Chicken *(page 10)* and Chicken with Cornbread Dumplings *(page 40).*

**Pictured on the back cover:** Apricot Pork Chop and Dressing *(page 44).*

ISBN: 0-7853-7148-6

Manufactured in China.

8 7 6 5 4 3 2 1

**Microwave Cooking:** Microwave ovens vary in wattage. Use the cooking times as guidelines and check for doneness before adding more time.

**Preparation/Cooking Times:** Preparation times are based on the approximate amount of time required to assemble the recipe before cooking, baking, chilling or serving. These times include preparation steps such as measuring, chopping and mixing. The fact that some preparations and cooking can be done simultaneously is taken into account. Preparation of optional ingredients and serving suggestions is not included.

# Contents

## Simply Delicious Foil Recipes

It's one of those days—everyone's on a different dinner schedule and you're wondering how you can avoid serving reheated, dried-out meals to the latecomers. Let foil packets come to the rescue! With packet cooking you can prepare individual servings, wrap them in foil and hold them in the refrigerator until you're ready to cook—no more reheating food for dinner stragglers. You can create delicious dinners easily and quickly and keep cleanup to a minimum when you cook in foil.

*Easy Foil Recipes* includes dozens of recipes for cooking or grilling in foil packets. In addition, discover the convenience of cooking in foil bags, lining baking pans with foil, and baking in foil cups. You'll be surprised how quick and easy foil cooking can be.

## Foil Packet Cooking

What is foil packet cooking? Wrap ingredients in foil to create packets, then cook them in a hot oven or on the grill. Packets can serve one or more. Recipes for one or two can be prepared in most toaster ovens, which will help to keep the kitchen cool and save energy. Vegetable packets can be tossed on the grill while the steaks or burgers are grilling. You'll love the convenience of this cooking method. Packets can be prepared ahead of time and cooked when needed. There are no pots and pans to scrub and the oven stays clean, too. You can even customize individual packets for fussy eaters—simply prepare one packet without the mushrooms that one family member dislikes.

## Packet Basics

◆ Measure and tear off a foil sheet(s) as directed in the recipe and place it on the countertop.

◆ Spray the foil with nonstick cooking spray or grease with butter or margarine as directed in the recipe. In most cases a light spraying is sufficient, but sticky or sugary foods may require a generous coating.

◆ Preheat the oven, toaster oven or the grill.

◆ Place the ingredients in the center of the foil sheets as the recipe directs.

◆ Wrap foil around the ingredients, leaving room for heat to circulate. Bring the two sides together above the food; double fold the foil and crimp to seal as shown in the top photograph.

◆ Double fold the remaining ends and crimp to seal the packet (bottom photograph).

◆ Place the foil packets on a baking sheet, toaster oven tray or a baking pan with 1-inch-high sides.

◆ Bake the packets on the baking sheet on center rack as directed. Or, slide the packets onto the grill.

◆ Remove packets from the oven. The foil packets will be very hot so use oven mitts when handling them. Carefully open one end of each packet to avoid the escaping steam. Allow some of the steam to escape before completely opening the packet. Check the food for doneness; rewrap and return to the oven if the food isn't completely cooked.

◆ Transfer the contents of the packets to serving plates or a serving dish. When cooking single-serve packets of food, you may eat right out of the packet if you wish.

**Double fold foil and crimp tightly to seal.**

**Double fold each end of packet and crimp tightly to seal.**

## Large Foil Bags

Foil bags large enough to hold a turkey are available at most supermarkets. Use these bags for large items such as turkeys, roasting chickens, beef roasts and pork roasts. Add vegetables to the bag and you have almost an entire meal prepared quickly and conveniently. Cleanup is easy, too.

**Crisscross the strips of foil like spokes of a wheel.**

**Pull foil strips up and over food.**

## Other Uses of Foil in the Kitchen

**Lining baking pans with foil:** When roasting meat or vegetables, first line the baking pan with foil to minimize cleanup. When baking bar cookies or brownies, line the baking pan with foil, allowing the edges of the foil sheet to overhang the edges of the pan. Grease the foil. After the bars or brownies are cool, simply lift them out of the pan using the foil.

**Lining cookie sheets with foil:** Place a sheet of foil on the cookie sheet when making cookies. Grease the foil if the recipe recommends greasing the cookie sheet. Place cookie dough on the foil and bake as directed. After removing cookies from the oven, slide the foil off the cookie sheet onto a wire rack or the countertop. Cool the cookie sheet and reuse it with another sheet of foil—the cookie sheet remains clean.

**Covering with foil:** Foil can be used to cover baking pans and casseroles during baking.

**Cooking in a slow cooker:** To easily lift a meatloaf or a casserole dish out of a slow cooker, make foil handles according to the following directions:

Cut three 18×3-inch strips of heavy-duty foil. Crisscross strips so they resemble the spokes of a wheel (top photograph). Place the dish or food in the center of the strips.

Pull foil strips up and over (bottom photograph) the food. Use the strips to lower the food into the slow cooker. Leave the strips in while you cook so you can easily lift them out again when finished cooking.

## Foil Bake Cups

Foil bake cups, like paper bake cups, are available in several sizes to line muffin pans when making muffins or cupcakes. The added bonus of foil bake cups is that they are rigid enough to be used without muffin pans. Simply place the bake cups on a baking sheet or in a baking pan with 1-inch sides.

## Disposable Foil Baking Pans

Disposable foil baking pans are readily available in many sizes. Use them in place of a roasting pan for a holiday turkey or a Sunday-supper roast. Use them for transporting your favorite dish to the next pot-luck dinner or picnic. There's no need to worry about searching for your casserole dish when the meal's over. Bake bar cookies, brownies and sheet cakes in disposable foil pans if you plan to ship them to friends or family or take them to a bake sale.

From tasty main dishes, like Spicy Pistachio Chicken and Apricot Pork Chops and Dressing, to taste-tempting side dishes and quick-to-fix meal finales, like Cinnamon-Raisin-Banana Bread Pudding and Easy Gingerbread, you'll discover a variety of recipes that will simplify dinner preparation whether you're cooking for one or an on-the-go family. So roll out the foil and enjoy an easy-to-make, home-cooked meal tonight!

◆ *Minutes to prepare, minutes to bake*

◆ *Make ahead, bake later*

◆ *Foil is versitale*

◆ *Cleanup is a snap!*

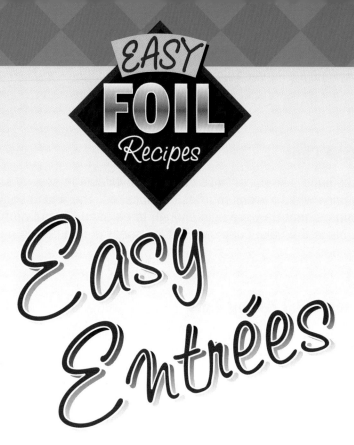

**EASY FOIL Recipes**

# Easy Entrées

## Spicy Pistachio Chicken

**4 TYSON® Individually Fresh Frozen® Boneless, Skinless Chicken Breasts**
**1 tablespoon unsalted butter, melted**
**¼ teaspoon cayenne pepper**
**¼ cup finely chopped pistachio nuts**
**1 tablespoon grated Parmesan cheese**
**1 tablespoon finely chopped green onion**

**PREP:** Preheat oven to 350°F. Prepare 4 pieces of foil large enough for each to hold 1 chicken breast. CLEAN: Wash hands. Place each breast on piece of foil. Brush chicken with melted butter and sprinkle with pepper. Wrap foil around chicken. CLEAN: Wash hands.

**COOK:** Place foil packets on cookie sheet; bake 35 minutes. Remove from oven; open foil and sprinkle pistachio nuts over chicken. Leave foil open and return to oven. Bake about 5 minutes or until internal juices of chicken run clear. (Or insert instant-read meat thermometer in thickest part of chicken. Temperature should read 170°F.)

**SERVE:** Remove chicken from foil and place on serving platter. Sprinkle chicken with Parmesan cheese and green onion.

**CHILL:** Refrigerate leftovers immediately.            *Makes 4 servings*

**Prep Time:** 10 minutes
**Cook Time:** 40 minutes

# Steak San Marino

¼ cup all-purpose flour
1 teaspoon salt
½ teaspoon black pepper
1¼ pounds beef sirloin steak, about ¾ inch thick, cut into 4 pieces
1 can (8 ounces) tomato sauce
1 carrot, chopped
½ onion, chopped
1 rib celery, chopped
1 teaspoon dried Italian seasoning
½ teaspoon Worcestershire sauce
  Hot cooked rice
4 sheets (18×12 inches) heavy-duty foil, lightly sprayed with nonstick
  cooking spray

**1.** Preheat oven to 450°F.

**2.** Combine flour, salt and pepper in small bowl. Coat beef in flour mixture. Place each piece of beef on foil. Combine tomato sauce, carrot, onion, celery, Italian seasoning and Worcestershire sauce in small bowl; pour a quarter of tomato sauce mixture over each piece of beef.

**3.** Double fold sides and ends of foil to seal packets, leaving head space for heat circulation. Place packets on baking sheet.

**4.** Bake 25 to 28 minutes or until beef is tender. Remove packets from oven. Carefully open one end of each packet to allow steam to escape. Open packets and transfer contents to serving plates. Serve steaks and sauce over rice.

*Makes 4 servings*

# Chicken Parmesan

**2 boneless skinless chicken breasts**
**2 sheets (18×12 inches) heavy-duty foil, lightly sprayed with nonstick cooking spray**
**Salt and black pepper**
**1 cup pasta sauce**
**½ cup chopped onion**
**8 slices zucchini, quartered**
**¼ cup (1 ounces) shredded mozzarella cheese**
**2 tablespoons grated Parmesan cheese**
**Hot cooked spaghetti or linguine (optional)**

**1.** Preheat toaster oven or oven to 450°F.

**2.** Place one chicken breast in center of each sheet of foil. Season to taste with salt and pepper.

**3.** Combine pasta sauce, onion and zucchini. Pour half of sauce mixture over each chicken breast. Sprinkle with cheeses. Double fold sides and ends of foil to seal packets, leaving head space for heat circulation. Place packets on toaster oven tray or baking sheet.

**4.** Bake 16 to 18 minutes until chicken is no longer pink in center. Remove from oven. Carefully open one end of each foil packet to allow steam to escape. Open packets and transfer contents to serving plates. Serve with spaghetti, if desired.                                    *Makes 2 servings*

# Turkey Loaf with Quick Foil Potatoes

**1 pound ground turkey breast (99% fat-free)**
**1¼ cups finely chopped onion, divided**
**½ cup finely chopped celery**
**2 eggs, beaten**
**6 tablespoons chili sauce, divided**
**1 clove garlic, minced**
**½ teaspoon salt**
  **Black pepper**
**4 cups frozen shredded hash brown potatoes**
  **Black pepper**
**2 tablespoons butter, cut into pieces**

**1.** Preheat oven to 375°F. Line 8×8-inch baking pan with foil; lightly spray with nonstick cooking spray. Set aside.

**2.** Combine turkey, ¾ cup onion, celery, eggs, 5 tablespoons chili sauce, garlic, salt and ⅛ teaspoon pepper in large bowl; mix well. Form turkey mixture into loaf in foil-lined baking pan. Spread remaining 1 tablespoon chili sauce on top of loaf.

**3.** Bake 50 to 55 minutes until juices run clear and thermometer inserted in center of loaf registers 170°F.

**4.** Meanwhile, lightly spray 1 sheet (18×12 inches) heavy-duty foil with cooking spray. Combine frozen hash browns, remaining ½ cup onion and pepper to taste in medium bowl; mix well.

**5.** Place hash brown mixture in center of foil. Dot with butter. Double fold sides and ends of foil to seal packet. Place packet on small baking sheet.

**6.** When turkey loaf has baked for 30 minutes, place foil packet in oven. Bake on baking sheet 25 minutes. Remove turkey loaf and foil packet from oven. Let stand 5 minutes. Carefully open one end of foil packet to allow steam to escape. Open packet and transfer mixture to serving plates. Serve with sliced turkey loaf.                                    *Makes 4 servings*

# Single-Serve Dijon & Honey Pork Chop

½ teaspoon LAWRY'S® Seasoned Salt
1 pork chop, cut ½ inch thick
½ cup sliced carrot
½ cup sliced celery
¼ cup sliced mushrooms
3 tablespoons LAWRY'S® Dijon & Honey Marinade with Lemon Juice

Sprinkle Seasoned Salt on both sides of chop. In small bowl, combine remaining ingredients; mix well. Place chop on 12×9-inch piece heavy-duty aluminum foil. Top chop with vegetable mixture. Fold foil to enclose; seal tightly. Freeze. Remove packet from freezer when ready to cook. Place packet seam side up on baking sheet. Bake in 425°F oven 1 hour or until chop is no longer pink in center. To serve, carefully remove chop and vegetables—they will be very hot. *Makes 1 serving*

**Serving Suggestion:** Place a potato in the oven at the same time as the pork chop packet—they'll be ready at the same time.

# Vegetarian Orzo & Feta Bake

**1 package (16 ounces) orzo pasta**
**1 can (4¼ ounces) chopped black olives, drained**
**2 cloves garlic, minced**
**1 sheet (24×18 inches) heavy-duty foil, lightly sprayed with nonstick cooking spray**
**1 can (about 14 ounces) diced Italian-style tomatoes**
**1 can (14 ounces) vegetable broth**
**2 tablespoons olive oil**
**6 to 8 ounces feta cheese, cut into ½-inch cubes**

**1.** Preheat oven to 450°F.

**2.** Combine orzo, olives and garlic in medium bowl. Place orzo mixture in center of foil sheet.

**3.** Fold sides of foil up around orzo mixture, but do not seal.

**4.** In same bowl, combine tomatoes with juice, broth and oil. Pour over orzo mixture. Top with cheese.

**5.** Double fold sides and ends of foil to seal packet, leaving head space for heat circulation. Place packet on baking sheet.

**6.** Bake 22 to 24 minutes or until pasta is tender. Remove from oven. Let stand 5 minutes. Open packet and transfer contents to serving plates

*Makes 6 servings (or 8 side dish servings)*

## Quick Tip

Using canned tomatoes that are already diced and canned olives that are already chopped is a great time saver when you are in a hurry to prepare dinner.

# Red Snapper Scampi

¼ **cup margarine or butter, softened**
1 **tablespoon white wine**
1½ **teaspoons minced garlic**
½ **teaspoon grated lemon peel**
⅛ **teaspoon black pepper**
1½ **pounds red snapper, orange roughy or grouper fillets**
    **(about 4 to 5 ounces each)**

**1.** Preheat oven to 450°F. Combine margarine, wine, garlic, lemon peel and pepper in small bowl; stir to blend.

**2.** Place fish on foil-lined shallow baking pan. Top with seasoned margarine. Bake 10 to 12 minutes or until fish begins to flake easily when tested with fork.
*Makes 4 servings*

**Tip:** Serve fish over mixed salad greens, if desired. Or, add sliced carrots, zucchini and bell pepper cut into matchstick-size strips to the fish in the baking pan for an easy vegetable side dish.

**Prep and Cook Time:** 12 minutes

# Garlicky Chicken Packets

1 **cup julienned carrots**
½ **cup sliced onion**
¼ **cup chopped fresh basil** *or* 1 **tablespoon dried basil leaves**
2 **tablespoons mayonnaise**
6 **cloves garlic, minced**
⅛ **teaspoon black pepper**
4 **boneless skinless chicken breast halves**

Cut foil into 4 (12-inch) squares. Fold squares in half.

Preheat oven to 400°F. Place a quarter of carrots and onion on 1 side of each foil square near fold. Combine basil, mayonnaise, garlic and pepper in small bowl; spread mixture on chicken. Place chicken, mayonnaise side up, on top of vegetables. Fold foil over chicken; seal by creasing and folding edges of foil. Place foil packets on baking sheet. Bake 20 to 25 minutes or until juices run clear and chicken is no longer pink in center.
*Makes 4 servings*

# That's Italian Meat Loaf

1 (8-ounce) can tomato sauce, divided
1 egg, lightly beaten
½ cup chopped onion
½ cup chopped green bell pepper
⅓ cup dry seasoned bread crumbs
2 tablespoons grated Parmesan cheese
½ teaspoon garlic powder
¼ teaspoon black pepper
1 pound ground beef
½ pound ground pork or veal
1 cup shredded Asiago cheese

**Slow Cooker Directions**

Reserve ⅓ cup tomato sauce; set aside in refrigerator. Combine remaining tomato sauce and egg in large bowl. Stir in onion, bell pepper, bread crumbs, Parmesan cheese, garlic powder and black pepper. Add ground beef and pork; mix well and shape into loaf.

Place meat loaf on foil strips (see page 8). Place in slow cooker. Cover and cook on LOW 8 to 10 hours or on HIGH 4 to 6 hours; internal temperature should read 170°F.

Spread meat loaf with reserved tomato sauce. Sprinkle with Asiago cheese. Cover and cook 15 minutes or until cheese is melted. Using foil strips, remove meat loaf from slow cooker. *Makes 8 servings*

# Make-Ahead Dill Chicken in Foil

**8 chicken thighs, skinned**
**1 teaspoon salt**
**½ teaspoon ground black pepper**
**½ cup butter or margarine, melted**
**2 tablespoons lemon juice**
**1 teaspoon dried dill weed**
   **Vegetable cooking spray**
**3 green onions, thinly sliced**
**1 cup thinly sliced carrots**
**6 ounces Swiss cheese, cut into 8 slices**

Sprinkle chicken thighs with salt and pepper. Combine butter, lemon juice and dill in small bowl. Cut four 12-inch squares of heavy-duty foil; coat each with cooking spray. Place 1 tablespoon dill-butter sauce on center of each foil square; place 2 chicken thighs on sauce. Divide onion and carrot slices evenly over chicken. Top each with additional 1 tablespoon sauce and 1 slice cheese. Fold foil into packets, sealing securely. Label, date and freeze chicken until ready to bake.* To serve, place frozen foil packets in baking pan and bake at 400°F 1 hour or until fork can be inserted into chicken with ease and juices run clear, not pink.    *Makes 4 servings*

*\*Chicken may be frozen for up to 9 months. If serving immediately without freezing, place foil packets in baking pan and bake at 400°F 35 to 40 minutes or until fork can be inserted into chicken with ease and juices run clear, not pink.*

*Favorite recipe from **National Chicken Council***

### Quick Tip

Preparing single-serve foil meal packets and freezing them for later use makes meal preparation a breeze. When you don't feel like preparing a meal for one or someone needs to eat early, just pull a packet out of the freezer, pop it into the oven and relax until dinner is ready.

# Fiesta Beef Enchiladas

6 ounces lean ground beef

¼ cup sliced green onions

1 teaspoon fresh minced or bottled garlic

1 cup (4 ounces) shredded reduced-fat Mexican cheese blend or Cheddar cheese, divided

¾ cup chopped tomato, divided

½ cup cold cooked white or brown rice

⅓ cup frozen corn, thawed

¼ cup salsa or picante sauce

6 (6- to 7-inch) corn tortillas

2 sheets (20×12 inches) heavy-duty foil, lightly sprayed with nonstick cooking spray

½ cup mild or hot red or green enchilada sauce

½ cup sliced romaine lettuce leaves

**1.** Preheat oven to 375°F. Cook ground beef in medium nonstick skillet over medium heat until no longer pink; drain. Add green onions and garlic; cook and stir 2 minutes.

**2.** Combine meat mixture, ¾ cup cheese, ½ cup tomato, rice, corn and salsa; mix well. Spoon mixture down center of tortillas. Roll up; place seam side down, on foil sheet, three to a sheet. Spoon enchilada sauce evenly over enchiladas.

**3.** Double fold sides and ends of foil to seal packets, leaving head space for heat circulation. Place packets on baking sheet.

**4.** Bake 15 minutes or until hot. Remove from oven. Carefully open packets. Sprinkle enchiladas with remaining ¼ cup cheese; bake 10 minutes more. Serve with lettuce and remaining ¼ cup tomato.

*Makes 2 servings*

**Prep Time:** 15 minutes
**Cook Time:** 25 minutes

# Chicken, Stuffing & Green Bean Bake

> 1 package (7 ounces) cubed herb-seasoned stuffing
> 4 sheets (18×12 inches) heavy-duty foil, lightly sprayed with nonstick cooking spray
> ½ cup chicken broth
> 3 cups frozen cut green beans
> 4 boneless skinless chicken breasts
> 1 cup chicken gravy
> ⅛ teaspoon black pepper

**1.** Preheat oven to 450°F.

**2.** Place a quarter of stuffing (1 scant cup) on one sheet of foil. Pour 2 tablespoons chicken broth over stuffing. Top stuffing with ¾ cup green beans. Place one chicken breast on top of beans. Combine gravy and pepper; pour ¼ cup over chicken.

**3.** Double fold sides and ends of foil to seal packets, leaving head space for heat circulation. Repeat with remaining stuffing, beans, chicken and gravy mixture to make three more packets. Place packets on baking sheet.

**4.** Bake 20 minutes or until chicken is no longer pink in center. Remove from oven. Carefully open one end of each packet to allow steam to escape. Open packets and transfer contents to serving plates. Serve with additional gravy, if desired. *Makes 4 servings*

# Barbara's Pork Chop Dinner

**Nonstick cooking spray**
**6 bone-in pork loin chops (¾ inch thick)**
**1 small onion, thinly sliced and separated into rings**
**6 sheets (18×12 inches) heavy-duty foil, lightly sprayed with nonstick cooking spray**
**6 medium red potatoes, unpeeled and cut into thin slices**
**1 can (10¾ ounces) condensed cream of chicken soup, undiluted**
**1 cup sliced fresh mushrooms**
**⅓ cup canned chicken broth**
**2 tablespoons Dijon mustard**
**2 cloves garlic, minced**
**½ teaspoon salt**
**½ teaspoon dried basil leaves**
**¼ teaspoon black pepper**
**Chopped fresh parsley**

**1.** Preheat oven to 450°F.

**2.** Spray large nonstick skillet with cooking spray. Brown pork chops quickly on both sides. Set aside.

**3.** Divide onion rings into 6 portions. Place one portion of onion rings on each sheet of foil. Top with potato slices.

**4.** Combine soup, mushrooms, chicken broth, mustard, garlic, salt, basil and pepper in medium bowl. Pour some of soup mixture over potatoes and onion. Top with pork chops and remaining soup mixture.

**5.** Double fold sides and ends of foil to seal packets, leaving head space for heat circulation. Place packets on baking sheet.

**6.** Bake 28 to 30 minutes or until potatoes are tender. Remove packets from oven. Carefully open one end of each packet to allow steam to escape. Open packets and transfer contents to serving plates. Sprinkle with parsley. *Makes 6 servings*

# Asian Beef & Orange Packets

2 cups instant rice
4 sheets (18×12 inches) heavy-duty foil, sprayed lightly with nonstick
    cooking spray
1 pound lean beef flank steak, cut into short, thin strips
½ teaspoon black pepper
1 green bell pepper, cut into thin strips
1 red bell pepper, cut in thin strips
½ cup teriyaki sauce
¼ cup orange marmalade
1 can (11 ounces) mandarin orange sections, drained
8 ice cubes
1 cup beef broth or water
1 green onion, sliced (optional)

**1.** Preheat oven to 450°F.

**2.** Place ½ cup rice in center of one sheet of foil. Divide beef strips into four equal portions. Arrange four beef strips on foil to enclose rice. Top with remainder of one portion of beef. Sprinkle with ⅛ teaspoon pepper.

**3.** Place a quarter of bell peppers on beef. Combine teriyaki sauce and marmalade in small bowl. Drizzle 1 tablespoon teriyaki sauce mixture over vegetables.

**4.** Arrange a quarter of orange sections around beef and rice. Place 2 ice cubes on top of vegetables. Fold up sides of foil and pour ¼ cup broth into packet.

**5.** Double fold sides and ends of foil to seal packet, leaving head space for heat circulation. Repeat with remaining rice, beef, bell peppers, sauce mixture, orange sections, ice cubes and broth to make three more packets. Place packets on baking sheet.

**6.** Bake 20 minutes or until beef and vegetables are tender. Remove from oven. Let stand 5 minutes. Open packets and transfer contents to serving plates. Garnish with green onion, if desired.          *Makes 4 servings*

# Sausage, Potato and Apple Bake

    3 tablespoons brown sugar
    1 tablespoon dried thyme leaves
    1 tablespoon dried oregano leaves
    ¼ cup dry white wine or apple cider
    2 tablespoons cider vinegar
    2 sweet potatoes (1½ to 2 pounds), peeled and cut into ¼-inch pieces
    2 apples, such as Fuji or McIntosh, peeled, cored and cut into ¼-inch pieces
    1 medium white onion, sliced into thin strips
    1 red bell pepper, cut into thin strips
    1 yellow bell pepper, cut into thin strips
    ½ cup golden raisins
    4 sheets (18×12 inches) heavy-duty foil, lightly sprayed with nonstick
        cooking spray
  1½ pounds smoked sausage, such as kielbasa or Polish sausage, sliced
        diagonally into ¼-inch pieces

**1.** Preheat oven to 450°F.

**2.** Combine sugar, thyme and oregano in large bowl. Stir in white wine and vinegar and stir until brown sugar is dissolved.

**3.** Add potatoes, apples, onion, bell peppers and raisins; toss to coat. Using slotted spoon, divide potato mixture evenly among foil sheets. Fold up sides of foil arround potato mixture.

**4.** Add sausage to bowl with remaining liquid; toss to coat. Divide sausage among four foil packets. Pour any remaining marinade over sausage mixture. Double fold sides and ends of foil to seal packets. Place packets on baking sheet.

**5.** Bake 20 minutes or until vegetables are tender. Remove packets from oven. Carefully open one end of each pack to allow steam to escape. Open packets and transfer contents to serving plates.        *Makes 4 servings*

# Chicken Divan

    1 cup instant rice
    2 sheets (18×12 inches) heavy-duty foil, lightly sprayed with nonstick
        cooking spray
    8 chicken tenders
 1½ cups broccoli florets
   ¼ cup chicken broth
    4 ice cubes
   ⅔ cup Alfredo pasta sauce
    2 tablespoons grated Parmesan cheese

**1.** Preheat oven to 450°F.

**2.** Place ½ cup rice in center of one sheet of foil. Place 4 chicken tenders on foil to enclose rice. Arrange half of broccoli on chicken. Pour 2 tablespoons chicken broth over rice. Top with two ice cubes.

**3.** Pour ⅓ cup sauce over chicken and broccoli. Sprinkle with 1 tablespoon cheese.

**4.** Double fold sides and ends of foil to seal packet, leaving head space for heat circulation. Repeat with remaining rice, chicken, broccoli, broth, ice cubes, sauce and cheese. Place packets on baking sheet.

**5.** Bake 15 minutes or until chicken is no longer pink in center. Remove from oven. Let stand 5 minutes. Open packets and transfer contents to serving plates. *Makes 2 servings*

## Summer Vegetable & Fish Bundles

**4 fish fillets (about 1 pound)**
**1 pound thinly sliced vegetables***
**1 envelope LIPTON® RECIPE SECRETS® Savory Herb with Garlic or Golden Onion Soup Mix**
**½ cup water**

*\*Use any combination of the following: thinly sliced mushrooms, zucchini, yellow squash or tomatoes.*

On two 18×18-inch pieces heavy-duty aluminum foil, divide fish equally; top with vegetables. Evenly pour savory herb with garlic soup mix blended with water over fish. Wrap foil loosely around fillets and vegetables, sealing edges airtight with double fold. Grill or broil seam side up 15 minutes or until fish flakes when tested with fork.          *Makes about 4 servings*

**Menu Suggestion:** Serve over hot cooked rice with Lipton® Iced Tea mixed with a splash of cranberry juice cocktail.

## Melted SPAM® & Cheese Poppy Seed Sandwiches

**½ cup butter or margarine, softened**
**3 tablespoons prepared mustard**
**1 tablespoon poppy seeds**
**8 slices cracked wheat bread**
**1 (12-ounce) can SPAM® Luncheon Meat, cut into 8 slices**
**4 (1-ounce) slices American cheese**

Heat oven to 375°F. In small bowl, combine butter, mustard and poppy seeds. Spread butter mixture on bread slices. Place 2 slices of SPAM® on each of 4 bread slices. Top SPAM® with 1 slice of cheese. Top with remaining 4 bread slices. Wrap sandwiches in foil. Bake 10 to 15 minutes or until cheese is melted.          *Makes 4 servings*

# Stuffed Bell Peppers

1 cup chopped fresh tomatoes
1 teaspoon chopped fresh cilantro
½ clove garlic, finely minced
½ teaspoon dried oregano leaves, divided
¼ teaspoon ground cumin
6 ounces lean ground round
½ cup cooked brown rice
¼ cup cholesterol-free egg substitute *or* 1 egg white
2 tablespoons finely chopped onion
¼ teaspoon salt
⅛ teaspoon black pepper
2 large bell peppers, any color, seeded and cut in half lengthwise
4 sheets (12×12 inches) heavy-duty foil, lightly sprayed with nonstick cooking spray

**1.** Preheat oven to 400°F.

**2.** Combine tomatoes, cilantro, garlic, ¼ teaspoon oregano and cumin in small bowl. Set aside.

**3.** Thoroughly combine beef, rice, egg substitute, onion, salt and black pepper in large bowl. Stir ⅔ cup of tomato mixture into beef mixture. Spoon filling evenly into pepper halves.

**4.** Place each pepper half on foil sheet. Double fold sides and edges to seal packets. Place packets on baking sheet.

**5.** Bake 30 minutes or until meat is longer pink and peppers are tender. Serve with remaining tomato salsa, if desired.          *Makes 4 servings*

# Steak & Gnocchi Bake

   **2 packages (1 pound each) gnocchi (frozen or dried)**
**½ pound button mushrooms**
   **2 pounds boneless beef sirloin (1 inch thick)**
      **Salt**
      **Black pepper**
**¼ to ⅓ cup grated Parmesan cheese**
   **3 tablespoons butter, softened to room temperature**
   **3 tablespoons whole-grain mustard**
**½ cup steak sauce**
   **6 to 8 sheets (18×12 inches) heavy-duty foil, lightly sprayed with nonstick
      cooking spray**

**1.** Preheat oven to 450°F. Cook gnocchi according to package directions;
drain.

**2.** Gently combine prepared gnocchi and mushrooms in medium bowl.

**3.** Cut steak across the grain into ⅛-inch slices. Season to taste with salt
and pepper.

**4.** Combine cheese, butter, mustard and steak sauce in small bowl.

**5.** Place one-sixth of gnocchi mixture in center of each sheet of foil. Divide
beef into six portions and arrange on top of gnocchi mixture. Divide
cheese mixture into six portions and place on beef.

**6.** Double fold sides and ends of foil to seal packets, leaving head space
for heat to circulation. Place packets on baking sheet.

**7.** Bake 12 to 15 minutes until beef is tender. Remove packets from oven.
Carefully open one end of each packet to allow steam to escape. Open
packets and transfer contents to serving plates.

*Makes 6 to 8 servings*

# Honey-Mustard Chicken with Sauerkraut & Spuds

**2 tablespoons stoneground mustard**
**1 tablespoon honey**
**2 boneless skinless chicken breasts**
**2 medium red potatoes, thinly sliced**
**2 sheets (18×12 inches) heavy-duty foil, lightly sprayed with nonstick cooking spray**
**¼ teaspoon salt**
**⅛ teaspoon black pepper**
**1½ cups fresh sauerkraut, divided**
**2 slices Swiss cheese**
**2 teaspoons minced fresh parsley *or* 1 teaspoon dried parsley flakes**
**Additional mustard**

**1.** Preheat toaster oven or oven to 450°F.

**2.** Combine mustard and honey in medium bowl. Add chicken and turn several times to coat with mustard mixture. Let stand 10 minutes.

**3.** Meanwhile, divide potato slices between foil sheets, overlapping slices to form a rectangle about size of chicken breast. Sprinkle potato slices with salt and pepper.

**4.** Place chicken on potato slices. Top with sauerkraut and cheese slices. Sprinkle with parsley.

**5.** Double fold sides and ends of foil to seal packets, leaving head space for heat circulation. Place packets on toaster oven tray or baking sheet. Bake 35 to 40 minutes or until meat is cooked and potatoes are tender.

**6.** Remove packets from oven. Carefully open one end of packets to allow steam to escape. Open packets and transfer contents to serving plates. Serve with additional mustard. *Makes 2 servings*

# Chicken with Cornbread Dumplings

    4 boneless skinless chicken breasts (about 1 to 1½ pounds)
    ½ cup chicken broth
    ½ cup half-and-half
    1 teaspoon salt
    1 teaspoon dried thyme leaves
    1 teaspoon black pepper
    ½ teaspoon dried sage leaves
    1 red bell pepper, diced
    1 can (8 ounces) cut green beans *or* 1 package (9 ounces) cut green beans,
        thawed and drained
    1 can (8 ounces) corn, drained
    4 sheets (12×12 inches) heavy-duty foil, lightly sprayed with nonstick
        cooking spray
    1 can (11½ ounces) refrigerated cornbread twists

**1.** Preheat oven to 450°F. Cut chicken breasts into ¾-inch cubes.

**2.** Mix chicken broth, half-and-half, salt, thyme, pepper and sage in large bowl. Add chicken, bell pepper, green beans and corn; stir to coat. Divide mixture evenly among four sheets of foil, reserving liquid. Fold up sides of foil arround chicken mixture.

**3.** Cut cornbread twists into pieces about 1 inch long; divide evenly among packets, placing cornbread pieces around outside edge of chicken mixture.

**4.** Adjust foil around chicken mixture, if necessary, leaving tops of packets open. Pour reserved liquid into foil packets, about 3 tablespoons per packet. Double fold sides and ends of foil to seal packets leaving head space for heat circulation. Place packets on baking sheet.

**5.** Bake 18 to 24 minutes or until chicken is no longer pink. Remove from oven. Carefully open one end of packets to allow steam to escape. Open packets and transfer contents to serving plates.          *Makes 4 servings*

**Note:** One (7-ounce) cornbread mix, prepared according to package directions, may be substituted for the refrigerated cornbread twists. Drop by rounded teaspoonfuls around edges of chicken mixture.

# Tilapia & Sweet Corn Baked in Foil

⅔ **cup fresh or frozen corn kernels**
¼ **cup finely chopped onion**
¼ **cup finely chopped red bell pepper**
2 **cloves garlic, minced**
1 **teaspoon chopped fresh rosemary** *or* ½ **teaspoon crushed dried rosemary, divided**
½ **teaspoon salt, divided**
¼ **to** ½ **teaspoon black pepper, divided**
2 **tilapia fillets (4 ounces each)**
1 **teaspoon olive oil**
2 **sheets (18×12 inches) heavy-duty foil, lightly sprayed with nonstick cooking spray**

**1.** Preheat toaster oven or oven to 400°F.

**2.** Combine corn, onion, bell pepper, garlic, ½ teaspoon fresh rosemary, ¼ teaspoon salt and half the black pepper in small bowl. Spoon half the corn mixture onto each sheet of foil, spreading out slightly.

**3.** Arrange tilapia fillets on top of corn mixture. Brush fish with oil; sprinkle with remaining ½ teaspoon fresh rosemary, ¼ teaspoon salt and black pepper.

**4.** Double fold sides and ends of foil to seal packets, leaving head space for heat circulation. Place packets on toaster oven tray or on baking sheet.

**5.** Bake 15 minutes or until fish is opaque throughout. Remove packets from oven. Carefully open one end of each packet to allow steam to escape. Open packets and transfer contents to serving plates.

*Makes 2 servings*

**Tip:** For a special flavor, roast corn and red bell pepper on foil-lined baking sheet, lightly sprayed with nonstick cooking spray, in 450°F oven for 15 minutes or until slightly brown, stirring once. Then proceed with recipe as directed above.

# Apricot Pork Chops and Dressing

1 box (6 ounces) herb-seasoned stuffing mix
½ cup dried apricots (about 16), quartered
6 sheets (18×12-inches) heavy-duty foil, lightly sprayed with nonstick
    cooking spray
6 bone-in pork chops, ½ inch thick
  Salt
  Black pepper
6 tablespoons apricot jam
1 bag (16 ounces) frozen green peas
3 cups matchstick carrots*

*Precut matchstick carrots are available in the produce section of large supermarkets.*

**1.** Preheat oven to 450°F. Prepare stuffing mix according to package directions; stir in apricots.

**2.** Place ½ cup stuffing mixture in center of one sheet of foil. Place 1 pork chop over stuffing mixture, pressing down slightly and shaping stuffing to conform to shape of chop. Sprinkle chop with salt and pepper. Spread 1 tablespoon apricot jam over pork chop.

**3.** Place ⅔ cup peas beside pork chop in curve of bone. Arrange ½ cup carrots around outside of chop.

**4.** Double fold sides and ends of foil to seal packet, leaving head space for heat circulation. Repeat with remaining stuffing mixture, pork chops, salt, pepper, jam and vegetables to make 5 more packets. Place packets on baking sheet.

**5.** Bake 25 to 26 minutes or until pork chops and vegetables are tender. Remove from oven. Carefully open one end of each packet to allow steam to escape. Open packets and transfer contents to serving plates.

*Makes 6 servings*

# Foil Baked Albacore

½ cup frozen peas
½ cup sliced carrot
½ cup sliced red or green bell pepper or zucchini
⅓ cup sliced onion
2 large mushrooms, sliced
1 (3-ounces) pouch of STARKIST® Solid White Tuna, drained
¼ cup bottled Italian dressing
   Salt and pepper to taste
1 large tomato, quartered
⅓ cup shredded Cheddar cheese (optional)

Combine vegetables; divide between 2 pieces (each 12 inches square) of heavy-duty foil. Divide tuna in half; mound over vegetables. Drizzle each serving with dressing; add salt and pepper. Add 2 tomato quarters to each serving; sprinkle with cheese, if desired. Fold foil into closed packet, sealing edges securely. Bake in 450°F oven 15 minutes or cook on barbecue until thoroughly heated.          *Makes 2 servings*

**Prep Time:** 25 minutes

# SPAM™ Hot Vegetable Salad Sandwiches

6 unsliced whole wheat buns or Kaiser rolls
1 (7-ounce) can SPAM® Luncheon Meat, cubed
1 cup (4 ounces) shredded Monterey Jack cheese
1 tomato, chopped
½ cup finely chopped broccoli
½ cup thinly sliced carrots
¼ cup chopped onion
2 tablespoons peppercorn ranch-style salad dressing

Heat oven to 350°F. Cut thin slice from top of each bun; reserve. Remove soft center from each bun, leaving ½-inch shell. Combine remaining ingredients. Spoon into buns, pressing filling into buns. Top with reserved bun tops. Wrap each sandwich tightly in aluminum foil. Bake 20 minutes or until thoroughly heated and cheese is melted.          *Makes 6 servings*

# Mediterranean Chicken

       4 boneless skinless chicken breasts
       4 sheets (18×12 inches) heavy-duty foil, lightly sprayed with nonstick
          cooking spray
     ½ teaspoon dried oregano leaves
       8 sun-dried tomatoes, cut into thin slivers
       2 jars (6 ounces each) quartered marinated artichoke hearts, drained
       1 can (about 4 ounces) sliced ripe olives, drained
   2⅔ cups cubed unpeeled baking potatoes
     ¼ cup Parmesan and garlic salad dressing
          Chopped parsley (optional)

**1.** Preheat oven to 450°F.

**2.** Place one chicken breast in center of one sheet of foil. Sprinkle with ⅛ teaspoon oregano. Top with quarter of tomatoes, artichokes and olives. Arrange ⅔ cup potatoes around the edge of chicken. Drizzle with 1 tablespoon salad dressing.

**3.** Double fold sides and ends of foil to seal packet, leaving head space for heat circulation. Repeat with remaining chicken, oregano, vegetables and dressing to make three more packets. Place packets on baking sheet.

**4.** Bake 25 minutes or until chicken is no longer pink in center. Remove packets from oven. Carefully open one end of each packet to allow steam to escape. Open packets and transfer contents to serving plates. Garnish, if desired, with chopped parsley.                    *Makes 4 servings*

## FOIL Recipes
# Spectacular Sides

## Broccoli in Cheese Sauce

    1 bag (16 ounces) frozen broccoli florets
    1 sheet (24×12 inches) heavy-duty foil, lightly sprayed with nonstick cooking
        spray
    1 can (10¾ ounces) condensed Cheddar cheese soup
    1 medium red or yellow bell pepper, cut into 1-inch pieces
    ¼ cup chopped onion
    ¼ cup milk
  1½ teaspoons Worcestershire sauce
    ⅛ teaspoon black pepper

**1.** Preheat oven to 450°F. Place frozen broccoli in center of sheet of foil. Fold foil up around broccoli to create pan.

**2.** Combine soup, bell pepper, onion, milk, Worcestershire sauce and black pepper in medium bowl; stir to blend. Pour over broccoli.

**3.** Double fold sides and ends of foil to seal packet, leaving head space for heat circulation. Place packet on baking sheet.

**4.** Bake 25 minutes or until vegetables are tender. Remove from oven. Carefully open one end of packet to allow steam to escape. Open packet and transfer broccoli mixture to serving bowl.          *Makes 6 servings*

# Oven Roasted Potatoes and Onions with Herbs

3 pounds unpeeled red potatoes, cut into 1½-inch cubes
1 large sweet onion, such as Vidalia or Walla Walla, coarsely chopped
3 tablespoons olive oil
2 tablespoons butter, melted, or bacon drippings
3 cloves garlic, minced
¾ teaspoon salt
¾ teaspoon black pepper
⅓ cup packed chopped mixed fresh herbs, such as basil, chives, parsley,
    oregano, rosemary, sage, tarragon and thyme

**1.** Preheat oven to 450°F. Arrange potatoes and onion in large shallow foil-lined roasting pan.

**2.** Combine oil, butter, garlic, salt and pepper in small bowl. Drizzle over potatoes and onion; toss well to combine.

**3.** Bake 30 minutes. Stir and bake 10 minutes more. Add herbs; toss well. Continue baking 10 to 15 minutes or until vegetables are tender and browned. Transfer to serving bowl. Garnish with fresh rosemary, if desired.

*Makes 6 servings*

# Dijon Garlic Bread

½ cup margarine, softened
¼ cup GREY POUPON® Dijon Mustard
1 teaspoon dried oregano leaves
1 clove garlic, crushed
1 (16-inch-long) loaf Italian bread

Preheat oven to 400°F. Blend margarine, mustard, oregano and garlic in small bowl. Slice bread crosswise into 16 slices, cutting ¾ of the way through. Spread margarine mixture on each cut side of bread. Wrap in foil. Bake 15 to 20 minutes or until heated through.

*Makes 16 servings*

# Zucchini Tomato Bake

**1 pound eggplant, coarsely chopped**
**2 cups zucchini slices**
**2 cups mushrooms slices**
**3 sheets (18×12 inches) heavy-duty foil, lightly sprayed with nonstick**
    **cooking spray**
**2 teaspoons olive oil**
**½ cup chopped onion**
**½ cup chopped fresh fennel (optional)**
**2 cloves garlic, minced**
**1 can (14½ ounces) whole tomatoes, undrained**
**1 tablespoon tomato paste**
**2 teaspoons dried basil leaves**
**1 teaspoon sugar**

**1.** Preheat oven to 400°F. Divide eggplant, zucchini and mushrooms into 3 portions. Arrange each portion on foil sheet.

**2.** Heat oil in small skillet over medium heat. Add onion, fennel, if desired, and garlic. Cook and stir 3 to 4 minutes or until onion is tender. Add tomatoes, tomato paste, basil and sugar. Cook and stir about 4 minutes or until sauce thickens.

**3.** Pour sauce over eggplant mixture. Double fold sides and ends of foil to seal packets leaving head space for heat circulation. Place packets on baking sheets. Bake 30 minutes. Remove from oven. Carefully open one end of each packet. Open and transfer contents to serving dish. Garnish as desired.

*Makes 6 servings*

# Sweet Potato and Apple Casserole

½ cup packed dark brown sugar
½ teaspoon ground cinnamon
¼ teaspoon ground mace or nutmeg
2 pounds fresh sweet potatoes, peeled, quartered and cored
1 sheet (24×18 inches) heavy-duty foil, generously sprayed with nonstick cooking spray
   Salt
3 tablespoons butter, divided
2 Granny Smith apples, peeled, quartered and cored
½ cup granola cereal

**1.** Preheat oven to 375°F. Place foil loosely in 8×8 or 9×9-inch square baking pan.

**2.** Mix brown sugar, cinnamon and mace in small bowl. Place ⅓ of potato slices in center of foil sheet. Sprinkle with salt to taste. Crumble half the sugar mixture over potatoes and dot with 1 tablespoon butter.

**3.** Slice each apple quarter into four wedges. Layer half the apples on top of potatoes. Repeat layers using potatoes, sugar mixture, butter and apples. Top with remaining potatoes and 1 tablespoon butter.

**4.** Double fold sides and ends of foil to seal packet, leaving head space for heat circulation. Place packet on baking sheet.

**5.** Bake 25 minutes. Remove packets from oven. Carefully open one end of packet to allow steam to escape. Open top of packet; spoon liquid in bottom of packet over potatoes. Sprinkle with granola; do not reseal packet. Bake 35 minutes more or until potatoes are fork-tender. Garnish, if desired.
*Makes 6 servings*

# Glazed Maple Acorn Squash

**1 large acorn or golden acorn squash**
**¼ cup water**
**2 tablespoons pure maple syrup**
**1 tablespoon margarine or butter, melted**
**¼ teaspoon ground cinnamon**
**1 sheet (24×18 inches) heavy-duty foil, lightly sprayed with nonstick cooking spray**

**1.** Preheat oven to 375°F.

**2.** Cut ends from squash. Cut squash crosswise into four equal slices. Discard seeds and membrane. Place squash on foil sheet. Fold sides of foil up around squash. Add water.

**3.** Double fold sides and ends of foil to seal packet, leaving head space for heat circulation. Place packet on baking sheet. Bake 30 minutes or until tender. Remove packet from oven.

**4.** Combine syrup, margarine and cinnamon in small bowl; mix well. Carefully open one end of packet to allow steam to escape and pour off water. Open top of packet. Brush squash with syrup mixture, letting excess pool in center of squash. Do not reseal packet.

**5.** Return packet to oven; bake 10 minutes or until syrup mixture is bubbly. Transfer contents of packet to serving dish. *Makes 4 servings*

# Green Beans with Savory Mushroom Sauce

**2 packages (10 ounces each) frozen French-style green beans, thawed**
**1 can (10¾ ounces) condensed cream of mushroom soup, undiluted**
**2 tablespoons dry vermouth or dry white wine**
**1½ cups mushrooms, sliced**
**½ teaspoon salt**
**½ teaspoon dried thyme leaves**
**¼ teaspoon black pepper**
**2 sheets (18×12 inches) heavy-duty foil, lightly sprayed with nonstick cooking spray**
**1 cup crushed prepared croutons or canned fried onion rings**

**1.** Preheat oven to 450°F. Mix all ingredients except foil and croutons in large bowl. Divide mixture between foil sheets. Double fold sides and ends of foil to seal packets. Place packets on baking sheet.

**2.** Bake 20 minutes or until hot. Remove from oven. Carefully open one end of each packet. Open packets and transfer contents to serving dish. Sprinkle with croutons. *Makes 6 to 8 servings*

# Chutney'd Squash Circles

**2 acorn squash (1 pound each)**
**1 sheet (18×18 inches) heavy-duty foil**
**2 tablespoons butter or margarine**
**½ cup prepared chutney**

**1.** Preheat oven to 400°F. Slice tip and stem end from squash. Scoop out and discard seeds. Cut squash crosswise into ¾-inch rings.

**2.** Center foil in 13×9-inch baking pan. Dot foil with butter and place squash on butter, slightly overlapping rings. Spoon chutney over slices and sprinkle with 2 tablespoons water. Double fold sides and ends of foil to seal packet, leaving head space for heat circulation.

**3.** Bake foil packet in baking pan 20 to 30 minutes until squash is fork-tender. Carefully open one end of packet to allow steam to escape. Open packet and transfer to warm serving plate. Pour pan drippings over squash. Garnish, if desired. *Makes 4 servings*

# Sweet & Sour Chicken

  **2 boneless skinless chicken breasts**
  **2 sheets (18×12 inches) heavy-duty foil, lightly sprayed with nonstick**
    **cooking spray**
    **Salt and black pepper**
  **½ medium green bell pepper, cut in short, thin strips**
  **½ medium red bell pepper, cut in short, thin strips**
  **¼ onion, cut in thin wedges**
  **½ cup drained canned pineapple chunks**
  **½ cup orange marmalade**
  **1 tablespoon white vinegar**
  **2 teaspoons cornstarch**
  **2 teaspoons soy sauce**
    **Hot cooked rice (optional)**

**1.** Prepare grill for direct cooking or preheat oven to 450°F.

**2.** Place one chicken breast in center of one sheet of foil. Season to taste with salt and pepper.

**3.** Place half of bell peppers and onion on chicken breast. Top with half of pineapple chunks.

**4.** Combine marmalade, vinegar, cornstarch and soy sauce in small bowl; stir until cornstarch is dissolved. Pour half over vegetables.

**5.** Double fold sides and ends of foil to seal packets, leaving head space for heat circulation. Repeat with remaining chicken, vegetables, pineapple and sauce mixture. Place packets on baking sheet.

**6.** Slide packets off baking sheet onto grid of covered grill. Grill 12 to 14 minutes over medium-high coals until chicken is no longer pink in center. Or, bake packets on baking sheet 16 to 18 minutes. Carefully open one end of each packet to allow steam to escape. Open packets and transfer mixture to serving plates. Serve with rice, if desired.

*Makes 2 servings*

# Grilled Paella

1½ to 2 pounds chicken wings or thighs
2 tablespoons plus ¼ cup extra-virgin olive oil, divided
   Salt and black pepper
1 pound garlicky sausage links, such as linguisa, chorizo or Italian
1 large onion, chopped
2 large red bell peppers, seeded and cut into thin strips
4 cloves garlic, minced
1 can (14 ounces) diced tomatoes, undrained
4 cups uncooked rice
16 tightly closed live mussels or clams,* scrubbed
½ pound large shrimp,* peeled and deveined with tails intact
1½ cups frozen peas
1 can (about 14 ounces) chicken broth
2 lemons, cut into wedges
1 oval disposable foil pan (about 17×13×3 inches)

*Seafood can be omitted; add an additional 1¼ to 1½ pounds chicken.

Brush chicken with 2 tablespoons oil; season with salt and black pepper. Grill chicken and sausage on covered grill over medium KINGSFORD® Briquets 15 to 20 minutes or until chicken juices run clear and sausage is no longer pink, turning every 5 minutes. Cut sausage into 2-inch pieces.

Heat remaining ¼ cup oil in large skillet over medium-high heat. Add onion, bell peppers and garlic; cook and stir 5 minutes or until vegetables are tender. Add tomatoes, 1½ teaspoons salt and ½ teaspoon black pepper; cook about 8 minutes until thick, stirring frequently. Combine onion mixture and rice in foil pan; spread evenly. Arrange chicken, sausage, seafood and peas over rice. Bring broth and 6 cups water to a boil in 3 quart saucepan. Place foil pan on grid over medium KINGSFORD® briquets; immediately pour boiling broth mixture over rice. Grill on covered grill about 20 minutes until liquid is absorbed. *Do not stir.* Cover with foil; let stand 10 minutes. Garnish with lemon wedges.

*Makes 8 to 10 servings*

# "Grilled" Tuna with Vegetables in Herb Butter

**4 pieces heavy-duty aluminum foil, each 18×12 inches**
**1 can (12 ounces) STARKIST® Tuna, drained and broken into chunks**
**1 cup slivered red or green bell pepper**
**1 cup slivered yellow squash or zucchini**
**1 cup pea pods, cut crosswise into halves**
**1 cup slivered carrots**
**4 green onions, cut into 2-inch slices**
    **Salt and black pepper to taste (optional)**

**Herb Butter**
**3 tablespoons butter or margarine, melted**
**1 tablespoon lemon or lime juice**
**1 clove garlic, minced**
**2 teaspoons dried tarragon leaves, crushed**
**1 teaspoon dried dill weed**

On each piece of foil, mound tuna, bell pepper, squash, pea pods, carrots and onions. Sprinkle with salt and black pepper.

For Herb Butter, in small bowl stir together butter, lemon juice, garlic, tarragon and dill. Drizzle over tuna and vegetables. Fold edges of each foil square together to make packets.

**To grill**
Place foil packets about 4 inches above hot coals. Grill for 10 to 12 minutes or until heated through, turning packets over halfway through grill time.

**To bake**
Place foil packets on baking sheet. Bake in preheated 450°F oven for 15 to 20 minutes or until heated through.

**To serve**
Cut an "X" on top of each packet; peel back foil.        *Makes 4 servings*

# Savory Grilled Potatoes in Foil

½ cup **MIRACLE WHIP®** Salad Dressing
1 teaspoon garlic powder *or* 3 garlic cloves, minced
½ teaspoon paprika
¼ teaspoon salt
¼ teaspoon black pepper
3 baking potatoes, cut into ¼-inch slices
1 large onion, sliced

**MIX** salad dressing and seasonings in large bowl until well blended. Add potatoes and onion; toss to coat.

**DIVIDE** potato mixture evenly among 6 (12-inch) square pieces of foil. Seal each to form packet. Place foil packets on grill over medium-hot coals.

**GRILL** covered, 25 to 30 minutes or until potatoes are tender.

*Makes 6 servings*

**Use Your Oven:** Assemble foil packets as directed. Place on center rack in oven. Bake at 425°F for 40 to 45 minutes or until potatoes are tender.

**Prep:** 15 minutes
**Grill:** 30 minutes

# Backyard S'Mores

2 milk chocolate bars (1.55 ounces each), cut in half
8 large marshmallows
4 whole graham crackers (8 squares)

Place each chocolate bar half and 2 marshmallows between 2 graham cracker squares. Wrap in lightly greased foil. Place on grill over medium-low **KINGSFORD®** Briquets about 3 to 5 minutes or until chocolate and marshmallows are melted. (Time will vary depending upon how hot coals are and whether grill is open or covered.)

*Makes 4 servings*

# Trout Stuffed with Fresh Mint and Oranges

**2 pan-dressed\* trout (1 to 1¼ pounds each)**
**½ teaspoon coarse salt, such as Kosher salt**
**1 orange, sliced**
**1 cup fresh mint leaves**
**1 sweet onion, sliced**

*\*A pan-dressed trout has been gutted and scaled with head and tail removed.*

**1.** Rinse trout under cold running water; pat dry with paper towels.

**2.** Sprinkle cavities of trout with salt; fill each with orange slices and mint. Cover each fish with onion slices.

**3.** Spray 2 large sheets of foil with nonstick cooking spray. Place 1 fish on each sheet. Double fold sides and ends of foil to seal packets, leaving head space for heat circulation.

**4.** Place foil packets, seam side down, directly on medium-hot coals; grill on covered grill 20 to 25 minutes or until trout flakes easily when tested with fork, turning once.

**5.** Carefully open one end of each foil packet to allow steam to escape. Remove and discard orange-mint stuffing. Serve immediately.

*Makes 6 servings*

# Cheddary Pull Apart Bread

**1 round loaf corn or sour dough bread (1 pound)***
**½ cup (1 stick) butter or margarine, melted**
**¼ cup *French's*® Classic Yellow® Mustard**
**½ teaspoon chili powder**
**½ teaspoon seasoned salt**
**¼ teaspoon garlic powder**
**1 cup (4 ounces) shredded Cheddar cheese**

*You may substitute one 12-inch loaf Italian bread for the corn bread.*

Cut bread into 1-inch slices, cutting about ⅔ of the way down through loaf. (Do not cut through bottom crust.) Turn bread ¼ turn and cut across slices in similar fashion. Combine butter, mustard and seasonings in small bowl until blended. Brush cut surfaces of bread with butter mixture. Spread bread "sticks" apart and sprinkle cheese inside. Wrap loaf in foil.

Place packet on grid. Cook over medium coals about 30 minutes or until bread is toasted and cheese melts. Pull bread "sticks" apart to serve.

*Makes about 8 servings*

**Prep Time:** 15 minutes
**Cook Time:** 30 minutes

### Quick Tip

This recipe may be prepared up to 12 hours ahead of time, wrapped in foil and refrigerated until 30 minutes before you plan to serve dinner. Simply add an additional five minutes to the grilling time.

# Vegetable-Topped Fish Pouches

    4 firm fish fillets, such as flounder, cod or halibut (about 1 pound)
    1 carrot, cut into very thin strips
    1 rib celery, cut into very thin strips
    1 medium red onion, cut into thin wedges
    1 medium zucchini or yellow squash, sliced
    8 mushrooms, sliced
    ½ cup (about 2 ounces) shredded Swiss cheese
    ½ cup WISH-BONE® Italian Dressing*

*\*Also terrific with Wish-Bone® Robusto Italian or Just 2 Good Italian Dressing.*

On four 18×9-inch pieces heavy-duty aluminum foil, divide fish equally.
Evenly top with vegetables, then cheese. Drizzle with Italian dressing. Wrap
foil loosely around fillets and vegetables, sealing edges airtight with
double fold. Let stand to marinate 15 minutes. Grill or broil pouches,
seam sides up, 15 minutes or until fish flakes easily with fork.

*Makes 4 servings*

# Lemon 'n' Dill Barbecued Corn-on-the-Cob

    6 medium (8 to 12 ounces each) unhusked whole ears corn
    3 tablespoons soft (50% reduced-calorie) margarine
      Grated peel of ½ SUNKIST® lemon
    1 tablespoon fresh squeezed juice from 1 SUNKIST® lemon
    1 tablespoon chopped fresh dill *or* 1 teaspoon dry dill weed
      Salt and white pepper to taste

Carefully pull back husks (do not detach) and remove silk from each ear of
corn. Rinse well in cold water. In small bowl, beat margarine, lemon peel
and lemon juice until well blended. Stir in dill. To prepare each ear of corn,
place on 12- to 16-inch-long piece of foil; brush corn with ⅙ of margarine
mixture. Sprinkle lightly with salt and pepper. Replace husks around corn;
individually wrap each securely in foil. Grill 6 inches above glowing coals or
on MEDIUM heat of gas barbecue 25 to 35 minutes, turning every
5 minutes. To serve, remove foil and cut off husks.     *Makes 6 servings*

# Baked Cinnamon Apples

4 medium Granny Smith or Rome Beauty apples
4 sheets (18×12 inches) heavy-duty foil, lightly sprayed with nonstick
   cooking spray
⅓ cup brown sugar, packed
¼ cup dried cranberries
½ teaspoon ground cinnamon
2 tablespoons butter, cut into 4 pieces
   Vanilla ice cream

**1.** Preheat oven to 450°F. Core apples. Using paring knife, trim off ½-inch strip around top of each apple. Place each apple in center of foil sheet.

**2.** Mix brown sugar, cranberries and cinnamon in small bowl. Fill apples with sugar mixture, sprinkling any excess around pared rim. Place 1 piece butter on sugar mixture; press gently.

**3.** Double fold sides and ends of foil to seal packets, leaving head space for heat circulation. Place packets on baking sheet.

**4.** Bake 20 minutes. Remove from oven. Carefully open foil packets; shape foil around apples. Bake 10 minutes more or until apples are tender. Remove from oven. Transfer apples to bowls; spoon remaining liquid over apples. Serve warm apples with ice cream.          *Makes 4 servings*

# Chocolate Frosted Peanut Butter Cupcakes

⅓ cup creamy or chunky peanut butter
⅓ cup butter, softened
½ cup granulated sugar
¼ cup firmly packed brown sugar
2 eggs
1 teaspoon vanilla
1¾ cups all-purpose flour
1½ teaspoons baking powder
½ teaspoon salt
1¼ cups milk
   **Peanut Butter Chocolate Frosting (recipe follows)**

**1.** Preheat oven to 350°F. Line 18 (2½-inch) muffin cups with foil or paper baking cups.

**2.** Beat peanut butter and butter at medium speed in large bowl of electric mixer until smooth; beat in sugars until fluffy. Beat in eggs and vanilla.

**3.** Combine flour, baking powder and salt in medium bowl. Add flour mixture to peanut butter mixture alternately with milk, beginning and ending with flour mixture.

**4.** Spoon batter into prepared muffin cups. Bake 23 to 25 minutes or until cupcakes spring back when touched and wooden pick inserted into centers comes out clean. Cool in pans on wire racks 10 minutes; remove from pans and cool completely.

**5.** Prepare Peanut Butter Chocolate Frosting. Frost each cupcake with frosting. *Makes 1½ dozen cupcakes*

**Peanut Butter Chocolate Frosting:** Combine 4 cups powdered sugar, ⅓ cup unsweetened cocoa powder, 4 tablespoons milk and 3 tablespoons creamy peanut butter; beat until well blended, adding additional milk, 1 tablespoon at a time, until desired consistency.

# Cinnamon-Raisin-Banana Bread Pudding

1 egg, beaten
2 tablespoons light brown sugar
1 tablespoon half-and-half or undiluated evaporated milk
¼ teaspoon cinnamon
¼ teaspoon vanilla
1 banana
1 tablespoon lemon juice
3 slices cinnamon-raisin bread
1 sheet (18×12 inches) heavy-duty foil, generously sprayed with nonstick cooking spray
2 teaspoons butter, softened and divided
2 tablespoons reduced-fat spreadable cream cheese, divided
1 tablespoon raisins
    Vanilla ice cream (optional)

**1.** Preheat oven or toaster oven to 350°F.

**2.** Mix together egg, brown sugar, half-and-half, cinnamon and vanilla in small bowl. Set aside.

**3.** Peel and chop banana; place in small bowl. Sprinkle with lemon juice and set aside.

**4.** Butter one side of one slice of bread with 1 teaspoon butter. Lay bread, buttered side down, on foil. Spread bread slice with 1 tablespoon cream cheese. Fold foil edges up to form close-fitting container around bread.

**5.** Spoon 2 tablespoons egg mixture onto bread slice. Arange half the bannana cubes on bread. Sprinkle with half the raisins. Spread remaining 1 tablespoon cream cheese on one side of one piece of bread. Place bread slice on bananas, cream cheese side down. Spoon 2 tablespoons egg mixture over bread slice. Top with remaining banana and raisins. Spread remaining 1 teaspoon butter on one side of remaining bread slice. Cut bread slice into cubes. Place bread cubes on banana. Drizzle remaining egg mixture over bread cubes. Do not seal foil container.

**6.** Place foil container on baking sheet. Bake 30 minutes or until pudding is set and top is golden brown and crusty. Remove from oven. Transfer bread pudding to serving plates. Serve with ice cream, if desired.

*Makes 2 to 3 servings*

# Spiced Pear with Vanilla Ice Cream

**1 sheet (18×12 inches) heavy-duty foil**
**2 teaspoons butter, softened**
**1 tablespoon light brown sugar**
**¼ teaspoon pumpkin pie spice**
**1 large Bosc pear, halved lengthwise and cored**
    **Lemon juice**
**2 scoops vanilla ice cream**

**1.** Preheat toaster oven or oven to 450°F. Coat center of foil with butter.

**2.** Combine sugar and pumpkin pie spice in small bowl. Sprinkle sugar mixture over butter. Sprinkle cut sides of pear halves with lemon juice. Place pear halves, cut side down, side by side on sugar mixture.

**3.** Double fold sides and ends of foil to seal foil packet, leaving head space for heat circulation. Place packet on toaster oven tray or baking sheet.

**4.** Bake 40 minutes or until pear halves are tender. Remove from oven. Let stand 15 minutes.

**5.** Open packet and transfer pear halves to serving plates. Spoon sauce over pears. Serve with ice cream. *Makes 2 servings*

### Quick Tip

An Anjou or Bartlett pear may be substituted for the Bosc pear, if desired. For a more compact packet, place pear halves side by side with the narrow tip of one half adjacent to the broad base of the other pear half.

# Easy Gingerbread

1 sheet (24×12 inches) heavy-duty foil
1 cup all-purpose flour
⅓ cup firmly packed brown sugar
1 teaspoon ground ginger
¾ teaspoon ground cinnamon
½ teaspoon baking soda
½ teaspoon baking powder
¼ teaspoon salt
¼ teaspoon ground cloves
1 egg
½ cup milk
⅓ cup melted butter
¼ cup unsulphured molasses
Powdered sugar (optional)

**1.** Preheat oven to 350°F. Center foil over 8×5×2½-inch loaf pan. Gently ease foil into pan. You will have a 1-inch overhang of foil on sides and a 5-inch overhang on ends. Generously spray foil with nonstick cooking spray.

**2.** Combine flour, brown sugar, ginger, cinnamon, baking soda, baking powder, salt and cloves in medium bowl; mix well.

**3.** In separate small bowl, beat egg. Stir in milk, butter and molasses until well mixed.

**4.** Add liquid mixture to dry ingredients; stir until smooth. Pour batter into foil-lined pan. Fold overhanging foil sides over batter to cover batter completely; crimp foil, leaving head space for cake as it rises.

**5.** Bake 45 minutes or until wooden pick inserted in center comes out clean. Remove from oven. Carefully open foil to allow steam to escape. Cool in pan on wire rack 10 to 15 minutes. Place serving plate over pan and invert gingerbread onto plate. Peel off foil.

**6.** Serve warm, or at room temperature sprinkled with powdered sugar, if desired.

*Makes 6 servings*

# Broiled Pineapple with Spiced Vanilla Sauce

    3 ounces reduced-fat cream cheese
    ¼ cup granulated sugar
    ¼ cup undiluted evaporated milk or half-and-half
    ¼ teaspoon pumpkin pie spice or Chinese 5-spice powder
    ¼ teaspoon vanilla
    1 sheet (14×12 inches) heavy-duty foil
    2 teaspoons butter
    2 thick, round slices fresh pineapple, skin and eyes trimmed
    1 tablespoon light brown sugar

**1.** Preheat broiler.

**2.** Place cream cheese, granulated sugar, milk, pumpkin pie spice and vanilla in food processor or blender; process until smooth. Refrigerate.

**3.** Coat center of foil sheet with butter. Place pineapple slices side by side on foil. Sprinkle with brown sugar. Fold up sides and ends of foil form container around pineapple, leaving top of container open. Place container on baking sheet.

**4.** Broil pineapple 4 inches from heat source 10 to 12 minutes until surface of pineapple is bubbling and flecked with brown. Watch pineapple closely during last 5 minutes of broiling to avoid burning.

**5.** Remove from oven. Transfer pineapple to serving plates. Serve immediately with cream cheese mixture. *Makes 2 servings*

# Chocolate Bread Pudding

1 sheet (12×12 inches) heavy-duty foil
4 slices firm-textured white bread
1 egg
1 tablespoon unsweetened cocoa powder
¾ cup milk
3 tablespoons sugar
1 teaspoon vanilla
⅛ teaspoon ground cinnamon
⅓ cup semisweet chocolate chips
   Whipped topping or sweetened whipped cream (optional)

**1.** Preheat oven to 350°F. Generously spray center of foil with nonstick cooking spray. Toast bread just enough to dry it, but not enough to brown it. Cool slightly and cut into cubes.

**2.** Beat egg in large bowl; whisk in cocoa until well blended. Stir in milk, sugar, vanilla and cinnamon. Add bread cubes and chocolate chips; stir until all bread cubes are moistened. Let stand until most of liquid is absorbed.

**3.** Place a portion of bread cube mixture in center of foil. Carefully shape foil up and around bread cubes to form bowl about 4-inches in diameter. Add remainder of bread cube mixture. Adjust foil, if necessary, leaving foil bowl open at top. Place foil bowl on baking sheet.

**4.** Bake 35 to 40 minutes or until set. Remove from oven. Cool 15 minutes. Serve warm or at room temperature garnished with whipped topping, if desired. *Makes 4 servings*

**Note:** If desired, chocolate milk may be substituted for milk and cocoa. Cinnamon bread may be substituted for white bread; omit ground cinnamon.

**The publisher would like to thank the companies and organizations listed below for the use of their recipes and photographs in this publication.**

ConAgra Grocery Products Company

Grey Poupon® Dijon Mustard

Hormel Foods, LLC

The Kingsford Products Company

Kraft Foods Holdings

Lawry's® Foods, Inc.

National Chicken Council

Reckitt Benckiser

StarKist® Seafood Company

Sunkist Growers

Tyson Foods, Inc.

Uncle Ben's Inc.

Unilever Bestfoods North America

**Apples**
    Baked Cinnamon Apples, 80
    Sausage, Potato and Apple Bake, 32
    Sweet Potato and Apple Casserole, 54
Apricot Pork Chops and Dressing, 44
Asian Beef & Orange Packets, 30

Backyard S'Mores, 74
Baked Cinnamon Apples, 80
Barbara's Pork Chop Dinner, 28
**Beef**
    Asian Beef & Orange Packets, 30
    Easy Pepper Steak & Rice, 70
    Fiesta Beef Enchiladas, 25
    Steak & Gnocchi Bake, 38
    Steak San Marino, 12
    Stuffed Bell Peppers, 3
    That's Italian Meat Loaf, 22
Broccoili in Cheese Sauce, 48
Broiled Pineaple with Spiced Vanilla Sauce, 89

Cheddary Pull Apart Bread, 78
**Chicken**
    Chicken, Stuffing & Green Bean Bake, 26
    Chicken Divan, 33
    Chicken Parmesan, 14
    Chicken with Cornbread Dumplings, 40
    Garlicky Chicken Packets, 20
    Grilled Paella, 66
    Honey-Mustard Chicken with Sauerkraut & Spuds, 39
    Make-Ahead Dill Chicken in Foil, 24
    Mediterranean Chicken, 47
    Spicy Pistachio Chicken, 10
    Sweet & Sour Chicken, 64
**Chocolate**
    Backyard S'Mores, 74
    Chocolate Bread Pudding, 90
    Chocolate Frosted Peanut Butter Cupcakes, 82
    Peanut Butter Chocolate Frosting, 82
Chutney'd Squash Circles, 58
Cinnamon-Raisin-Banana Bread Pudding, 84
**Corn**
    Chicken with Cornbread Dumplings, 40
    Garden Fresh Vegetable Bundles, 61
    Lemon 'n' Dill Barbecued Corn-on-the-Cob, 79
    Tilapia & Sweet Corn Baked in Foil, 42

Dijon Garlic Bread, 50

Easy Gingerbread, 88
Easy Pepper Steak & Rice, 70

Fiesta Beef Enchiladas, 25
Foil Baked Albacore, 46

Garden Fresh Vegetable Bundles, 61
Garlicky Chicken Packets, 20
Glazed Maple Acorn Squash, 56
Green Beans with Savory Mushroom Sauce, 58
Grilled Banana Squash with Rum & Brown Sugar, 71
Grilled Paella, 66
Grilled Potato Salad, 62
Grilled Sweet Potato Packets with Pecan Butter, 71
"Grilled" Tuna with Vegetables in Herb Butter, 68

Herbed Mushroom Vegetable Medley, 72
Honey-Mustard Chicken with Sauerkraut & Spuds, 39

Lemon 'n' Dill Barbecued Corn-on-the-Cob, 79

Make-Ahead Dill Chicken in Foil, 24
Mediterranean Chicken, 47
Melted SPAM® & Cheese Poppy Seed Sandwiches, 34
**Mushrooms**
    Barbara's Pork Chop Dinner, 28
    Green Beans with Savory Mushroom Sauce, 58
    Herbed Mushroom Vegetable Medley, 72
    Steak & Gnocchi Bake, 38
    Vegetable-Topped Fish Pouches, 79
    Zucchini Tomato Bake, 52

**Nuts**
    Grilled Sweet Potato Packets with Pecan Butter, 71
    Peanut Butter Chocolate Frosting, 82
    Spicy Pistachio Chicken, 10

Oven Roasted Potatoes and Onions with Herbs, 50

**Pasta**
    Steak & Gnocchi Bake, 38
    Vegetarian Orzo & Feta Bake, 18

# METRIC CONVERSION CHART

### VOLUME MEASUREMENTS (dry)

1/8 teaspoon = 0.5 mL
1/4 teaspoon = 1 mL
1/2 teaspoon = 2 mL
3/4 teaspoon = 4 mL
1 teaspoon = 5 mL
1 tablespoon = 15 mL
2 tablespoons = 30 mL
1/4 cup = 60 mL
1/3 cup = 75 mL
1/2 cup = 125 mL
2/3 cup = 150 mL
3/4 cup = 175 mL
1 cup = 250 mL
2 cups = 1 pint = 500 mL
3 cups = 750 mL
4 cups = 1 quart = 1 L

### VOLUME MEASUREMENTS (fluid)

1 fluid ounce (2 tablespoons) = 30 mL
4 fluid ounces (1/2 cup) = 125 mL
8 fluid ounces (1 cup) = 250 mL
12 fluid ounces (1 1/2 cups) = 375 mL
16 fluid ounces (2 cups) = 500 mL

### WEIGHTS (mass)

1/2 ounce = 15 g
1 ounce = 30 g
3 ounces = 90 g
4 ounces = 120 g
8 ounces = 225 g
10 ounces = 285 g
12 ounces = 360 g
16 ounces = 1 pound = 450 g

### DIMENSIONS

1/16 inch = 2 mm
1/8 inch = 3 mm
1/4 inch = 6 mm
1/2 inch = 1.5 cm
3/4 inch = 2 cm
1 inch = 2.5 cm

### OVEN TEMPERATURES

250°F = 120°C
275°F = 140°C
300°F = 150°C
325°F = 160°C
350°F = 180°C
375°F = 190°C
400°F = 200°C
425°F = 220°C
450°F = 230°C

### BAKING PAN SIZES

| Utensil | Size in Inches/Quarts | Metric Volume | Size in Centimeters |
|---|---|---|---|
| Baking or Cake Pan (square or rectangular) | 8×8×2 | 2 L | 20×20×5 |
| | 9×9×2 | 2.5 L | 23×23×5 |
| | 12×8×2 | 3 L | 30×20×5 |
| | 13×9×2 | 3.5 L | 33×23×5 |
| Loaf Pan | 8×4×3 | 1.5 L | 20×10×7 |
| | 9×5×3 | 2 L | 23×13×7 |
| Round Layer Cake Pan | 8×1½ | 1.2 L | 20×4 |
| | 9×1½ | 1.5 L | 23×4 |
| Pie Plate | 8×1¼ | 750 mL | 20×3 |
| | 9×1¼ | 1 L | 23×3 |
| Baking Dish or Casserole | 1 quart | 1 L | — |
| | 1½ quart | 1.5 L | — |
| | 2 quart | 2 L | — |